LANG'S RETURN

A MORGAN'S RUN ROMANCE

M. LEE PRESCOTT

Published by Mt. Hope Press

This book is a work of fiction. Names, characters, places, and events are products of the author's imagination or are used fictitiously. Any resemblance to actual people (alive or deceased), locales, or events is entirely coincidental

For my family and friends, with love.

could block out the horror of several few hours earlier when she had come home to the condo she shared with Bill and found him in bed with another woman.

She had wanted to surprise him, and that she did. He had just returned from two weeks researching in Monument National Park, and they had arranged to meet at the ranch for dinner. But the morning had been slow, and Beth had missed her lover and dearest friend. If she took the afternoon off, maybe they would call and make an excuse not to dine with the family. She wanted him all to herself. The recollection brought on a fresh spate of tears. Suddenly a clean, ironed handkerchief appeared, which she took with a muffled, "Thank you."

"Want to talk about it?"

"No."

"Might help."

"I doubt it. Besides, I'm not in the habit of unburdening myself to anyone, especially to a stranger."

"Oh, now that hurts. Stranger? We practically grew up together."

"Not that you paid me the slightest attention."

If you'd looked like you do now, I might have, darlin'. My mistake. "Have a lovers' quarrel, did you?"

"Oh, what the hell? What does it matter anyway? The whole valley will know by morning. I had the good luck to come home for a surprise reunion with my boyfriend, only to find him in bed with one of his grad students. Let's just say they weren't sleeping. My mind will no doubt hold on to that image forever."

"I'm sorry. He's an ass."

"Maybe."

"Maybe? In your house? With a student? What is he, a professor?"

She nodded, peering over at the strong jaw that now appeared clenched in anger. *My champion,* she thought. "Yes, he's a biology professor at U of A."

"How long have you been together?"

"Seven years."

"That sucks."

"Big time."

"Where am I taking you?"

"The big house. I'm running home to mommy and daddy with my tail between my legs. Pathetic, huh?"

"When you have parents like yours, it's the right move."

He turned in at the gate, "Morgan's Run" emblazoned above it, and the Rover headed up the rise to the huge farmhouse.

"With any luck, no one will be around, and I can slink up to my room unnoticed."

She appeared to get her wish. As he helped her carry her things to the wide porch, they were uninterrupted. "That's fine, right here. Thank you."

She smiled and extended her hand, which he took, saddened to feel her trembling and the coldness that had crept over her.

"Take care, Beth Morgan. I'll see you around."

"Lucky you."

She withdrew her hand and disappeared into the house. As Lang headed back to the Rover, his heart felt heavy, his body cold and empty without her touch.

CHAPTER 2

Beth watched the Rover disappear over the rise and turn away. The encounter with Lang Dillon had distracted her, but now the crushing hurt of the last few hours bore down. In shock at the cataclysmic and abrupt change in direction her life had taken in only a few hours, the usually stoic Morgan daughter sat in a porch rocker and breathed deeply, glad to be home.

She had spoken only five words to Bill: "Get out while I pack." He had complied, his lover following at his heels. She had raced around the condo, throwing as many of her belongings into bags and boxes as she could. *What a nightmare.* She bent over, head in hands, and sobbed.

Always the quiet, solid Morgan, Beth had never been given to outbursts or strong displays of emotion. She could not remember the last time she had cried. Solid, dependable Beth had escaped ranch living to reside in Tucson with her beloved Bill, her former professor. They had made a comfortable life for themselves away from the ranch where she worked every day. Their activities mostly centered around Bill's university friends, which suited her just fine.

Growing up, her siblings were constantly surrounded by friends, but Beth had few. Bookish and shy, she spent most of her free time with a nose in her books or helping out on the ranch's vast farm. Morgan's Run had the largest organic farm in the state, which she now ran with her sister, Ruthie, and workers who had been surrogate parents to them both. Bill and the farm were her entire life.

She met Bill her first week at the University of Arizona when she enrolled in his Biology 101, a huge first-year class with over a hundred students. She had remained after class on that first day to ask Professor Sampson to sign her gray card to allow her into the course. He had signed it and asked if she wanted to go for coffee. It was Bill's first year of teaching. Shy and reserved like herself, he sensed a kindred spirit in the lovely young woman eight years his junior. They often laughed about that encounter and how Bill had not yet learned to set boundaries between himself and students.

They had dated on and off for three years before he asked her to move in with him senior year. Her parents had screamed, yelled, and begged her to stay in the dorm, but once she made up her mind, Beth could seldom be dissuaded. Five years ago, they had moved from Bill's faculty apartment to a condo near the foothills, with hiking trails right outside their door. They had purchased it together, and she groaned thinking about the headache of dividing their very mingled assets, which included joint checking and savings accounts, the condo, and land they had purchased to the north, near Flagstaff. Their intention had been to build a vacation cabin in the next few years and spend a good part of each summer in the mountains they both loved.

She moaned as fresh sobs wracked her slender frame. This was how her older brother found her, head in hands, crying. Ben could not remember his sister crying since she was ten and fell off her horse, and even then there had not been audible wailing, just a few tears streaking her face.

"Hey, Beth, what's going on?"

He took the porch steps in one stride and knelt in front of his sibling. Of all the Morgan children, Beth and Ben were closest, their relationship largely unspoken, borne by an appreciation for and understanding of each other. However, dealing with uncontrollable weeping was uncharted territory for the dust-covered cowboy, who had stopped in at the house for his father's map box.

She gazed up at her handsome brother, his chestnut eyes full of concern. He had pushed his hat back, and a line of grime and sweat crisscrossed his brow, his dark brown hair flecked with red dust. "Where have you been?"

"Harley and I have been breaking in a new mustang. Morning was a little wilder than we anticipated." He meant Harley Langdon, his oldest friend, with whom he ran the ranch's stables. He smiled his hundred-watt smile that made

CHAPTER 3

As Lang drove through the gates of his parents' ranch, past the Saguaro Valley Winery sign, he wondered if this visit was a mistake. It would be great to see Rosie, his sister, but since his wild high school days, his relationship with his parents had never been easy. Once he left for Middlebury, he had never returned to the Valley. Summers he found jobs in his beloved Green Mountains, or on the Maine coast. Now, he lived in Cambridge, in a house he had renovated from roof to basement, a home where he was comfortable, surrounded by friends and colleagues he enjoyed. No lady love at the present, but the breakup with Priscilla, his girlfriend since junior year at Middlebury, had been tough. It was almost nine months, but he wasn't ready to take the plunge again.

It had been his fault, or so he thought. She wanted commitment, marriage, and kids and he wasn't ready for any of that. In truth, life with Cilla had been comfortable, but boring. They had grown apart and seemed to want different things, and their interests could not have been more different. She loved fashion shows, cocktail parties, and the social life of Beacon Hill, where she had grown up. He made every excuse in the book to get out of the continuous party and dinner invitations she threw at him. He loved the outdoors; she hated it. He wanted to buy land in the Berkshires or Vermont and start a small farm. Cilla told him he was crazy and said that "four years in the boonies was enough to last a lifetime."

He missed Cilla's touch, her beautiful smile on a Sunday morning as they woke and made languid love before starting their day. Often they spent the entire morning in bed, reading papers, eating sumptuous breakfasts, and making love again before rising for showers and maybe a walk along the Charles. No sense dwelling on the past. Cilla had moved on, and he should, too. He had heard through friends that she was in a serious relationship with a hedge fund guy and that their engagement was imminent.

"Lang! You're here. Finally!" Martha Dillon greeted him with open arms.

She looked well, her snow-white hair carefully coiffed. Dressed in her signature A-line skirt and white eyelet top, his mother looked a decade younger than her sixty-five years. As he hugged her, Lang was genuinely glad he had come, for her sake.

"Hey, Mom. You look like a million bucks, as always."

"Oh, pish tush, you're such a liar. Come on in the house and we'll have Neecy get you a nice, cool drink."

Neecy Rodriquez waved from the porch, her smooth, flawless skin, brown as a berry. Just this side of plump, Neecy had grown up on the ranch, played with Lang and his sister Rose, and now acted as housekeeper. The Dillons also had a chef, Jon Wilson, who had come to the Valley from Laguna Beach, California. A chef, not a cook, the attractive forty-something man had always wanted to live and work at a winery. He had a boyfriend in Tucson, but seemed quite content living above the garage, in a lovely apartment Martha had decorated especially for him. The Dillons were very generous to their help. Neecy lived in one of the property's guesthouses with her husband, Manual, who worked at the winery.

"Hey, Neecy, lookin' good!" Lang called as he pulled his two bags from the back of the Rover. He was rewarded by a huge grin. Neecy had always had a major crush on gorgeous, unattainable Lang Dillon.

"After your phone call this morning, we expected you earlier, darling," Martha said.

"Had a slight detour."

"Oh?"

"Beth Morgan was broken down on the road a couple of miles out of town. Stopped to help her, then dropped her at the ranch."

"That was sweet of you. Did she remember you?"

He laughed. "How could she forget? I was probably one of her worst tormenters before I left town."

"Pish tush, she's a tough one."

"Not today." He related the circumstances of their meeting and an abbreviated version of Beth's breakup and decision to move home.

"How horrible for her. That Bill always seemed like such a nice man."

"Well, he's a first-class jerk, if you ask me. Cheating on a beautiful woman like that after ten years together."

"Has it been that long? Dear me. Would you call Beth Morgan beautiful? I've always thought of her as rather a plain Jane, especially alongside her gorgeous brothers, and perky little Ruthie."

That's because you never really looked at her, he thought, but he let his mother's comment go. No sense in starting an argument five minutes after his homecoming. He gave Neecy a hug, then followed the two women into the house.

"We've put you in your old room, refurbished since the last time you saw it. Hope that's okay? If you'd rather use one of the other bedrooms, that's fine, too."

"My old room sounds good to me. I'll throw these things in and come down for a drink."

Without waiting for his mother's reply, he took the stairs two at a time, already feeling suffocated in the vast, overdecorated ranch house. His bedroom had been painted, the walls a soft red adobe hue. A patchwork quilt in greens, reds, and golds adorned the four-poster bed, and the new rough-hewn oak furnishings included a dresser, two bedside tables, and a desk. The room had a solid, lived-in look, although, with four additional guest rooms, he doubted that anyone had slept in it since he left. The bathroom had also been redone in deep red adobe, accented with colorful Mexican tiles in blue, white, and red. He stepped in, splashed water on his face, and stared out the window to a view of the acres and acres of grapevines as far as the eye could see. He was home, or in his parents' home, and all he could think of was his real home in Cambridge, and the beautiful, sad-eyed woman he had rescued moments earlier.

Absently she stared out the window, remembering Lang Dillon's sky-blue eyes. She would have given anything to get lost in those eyes and forget the horror of today. "It was kind of him to stop. I can't remember if I even thanked him, I was so out of it."

"Well, you'll have your chance tonight. I expect his folks'll drag him along to dinner. Mama was going to call over and let Martha know he was welcome."

"Oh, Dad, I don't feel like seeing anyone tonight."

"Up to you, darlin'. Carmela can bring you a tray or you can join us. It's not for a couple of hours. You think on it. Might take your mind off things."

She leaned against the strong shoulder, soaking up her father's warmth. "Thanks, Dad."

"'Tis nothin', darlin'. There ain't anything I wouldn't do for my darlin' girl. Hope you know that. Haven't seen you cry since Nona died. Good to let it all out."

She nodded against his chest.

"And, Bethie. Remember, I've got lots of friends in the Rangers. One phone call and I could have Sampson relocated, if you know what I mean."

She chuckled. "No Rangers, no relocating, no brothers, no lynchings, please!"

He kissed the top of her head. "Well, best get down and see what your mama's up to. Glad you're home, sweetheart. Good for your mama and me to have our two girls under the same roof again."

As if on cue, they heard Beth's youngest sibling, Ruthie's voice call out from below. "Hey, anyone home? Just saw Beth's truck on the Gila. Any idea where she is?"

"You stay put," he said, patting Beth's arm. "I'll fend her off."

"Thanks, Dad."

*****

Jaybo Dillon eyed his oldest, sitting with his mother on the terrace, iced tea in hand. "So our city slicker has returned."

"Hey, Dad." Lang rose and came to hug his father.

Years of rich eating and a fondness for the bottle had left Jay Dillon florid-faced and on the stocky side. His jeans hung way below a protruding belly, and he walked with the bow-legged gait of a tall, seasoned cowboy. At six-one, he towered over his wife, but not his son.

"Good to have you, Lang. Means a lot to your mother."

Martha winked at her son behind her husband's back. Both knew it meant the world to Jaybo Dillon, too, to have his son home. "Rose says she'll meet us at Morgan's Run. She's running late at the clinic."

"I'm not sure I should go tonight, guys," he said, looking from one parent to the other. "Feel like I'm horning in."

"Nonsense. Leonora Morgan called and specifically invited you, silly. Didn't I tell you that?"

"Yes, but—"

"No buts about it, son. Your mother and I won't go unless you do. Now, let's change the subject. Let me get a cold beer. Then I want to hear all about life in the big city."

Moments later, his father returned with two beers and handed one to him and a glass of white wine to his mother. Lang noticed she set the wine aside and watched his father, perhaps gauging how much he had already had to drink throughout the day. *Nothing changes,* he thought sadly. *Nothing except Beth Morgan, who has morphed from a plain ugly duckling into a lithe, lovely swan.* The prospect of seeing her in a few hours buoyed his spirits as he braced himself for the onslaught of questions.

CHAPTER 5

Maggie, Ben, and Emma arrived first and greeted Beth, Ruthie, and their parents on the back terrace. Emma, almost five now, had learned to walk again after surgery to correct her injuries from a car accident. It had been nothing short of a miracle. All the Morgan siblings and parents had helped with her therapy and rehabilitation. Emma was Ben and Maggie's child, conceived after a night of passion, right before Ben left for California. When he returned to Saguaro Valley a year ago and discovered he had a daughter, his life changed forever. He also got reacquainted with Maggie Williams, and in the process gave his heart to mother and child.

"Hey, Emmie! Don't you look pretty." Beth opened her arms to her beloved niece, who was dressed in a yellow sleeveless sundress. She ran her fingers through the child's dark brown curls, loving the scent of jasmine and lime.

Emma raced off to hug her grandfather, and Maggie came forward and hugged Beth. His brother's wife looked gorgeous as always, her long auburn hair falling over her slender, tanned shoulders. Her pale blue dress hugged every curve, including her baby bump. Just last week, Ben had announced she was four months pregnant.

"Hey, Beth. I'm so sorry. If there's anything we can do, please let us know."

"Thanks, Mags. I'll figure it out. I might like a mental health break now and then while in residence here," she whispered. "If you know what I mean."

"Absolutely. You know the door is always open."

Beth glanced over to find her brother staring fondly at them. He grabbed a beer and came to hug her. "Two of my favorite women," he said, rubbing Maggie's bump.

"I tell you what," Maggie said. "Dad's dropping Em at school tomorrow. Things are slow at the stables. I bet my bosses would give me the morning off, and you and I could go in to Gracie's for breakfast, maybe take a hike or a ride? Could you spare the time from the farm?"

"Not all day, but a couple of hours. I'd like that. Thanks, Mags. That is, if the boss says it's okay?"

"Well, since Mother Hen won't let me do half of my usual work with this," she said, patting her stomach, "I imagine he can spare me, right, Boss?"

"Absolutely. I'll square it with Harley. Will you be back in time for lessons?"

"Count on it, cowboy." Maggie winked at Beth. "I'll pick you up around nine. Sound good?"

"Perfect. I'll let Ruthie know."

"Know what? Did I hear my name?"

Their youngest sibling came up from behind, poking her brother.

"Hey, Shortcake," Ben said.

Their freckle-faced sibling jabbed him, tossing back her red curls in a mock huff. "Don't call me that, you bully."

"Can you cover for me tomorrow morning, sis? Maggie and I are going into town for a couple of hours."

For an instant, hurt at being left out of the girls' outing registered in Ruthie's pale blue eyes. Just as quickly, she recovered. Like the rest of them, she saw Beth was in pain and would do anything to take it away. "Got you covered, sis. All went fine today, too, by the way. And Raoul was just heading out to get your truck when Lang Dillon magically appeared, towing it with one of the winery trucks. Gosh, he's one gorgeous hunk of man, isn't he?"

"Is he now?" Maggie asked, watching Beth's face turn red. She had only vague recollections of Lang Dillon from childhood. The words *wild* and *rebellious* came to mind.

"You'll see for yourself soon enough. He's coming to dinner. Rose, too. In fact, speak of the devil." Ruthie gazed behind them as Lang and his parents greeted

Leonora and Ben Senior. Right behind them, Harley Langdon stepped onto the terrace, tipping his hat first to his hosts, then his friends before removing it and setting it on the terrace wall. Ruthie's jaw dropped. "No one told me Harley was coming."

"I invited him," Ben said, grinning from ear to ear. Ruthie had been in love with Harley since she was ten. She was currently dating a CPA from Tucson, whom she'd met online, but the romance seemed to be waning. No telling what Harley was up to. He kept his love life very private, but truth be told, he was as in love with Ruthie Morgan as she was with him. When Ben asked him about it, he claimed she was too young for him, and he was waiting for her to grow up.

"Well, you mighta told me!" Ruthie jabbed her brother again.

"What's the fun in that?"

After kissing Leonora Morgan and shaking hands with the others, Harley accepted a beer from Raoul, Carmela's husband, who stood manning the grill as he did at most Morgan dinner parties. Then he strolled as only Harley could to join them, a twinkle in his eye.

Ben clinked bottles with his best friend. "Hey, buddy."

"Hey, yourself. Ladies, I see we have a new cock in the henhouse," he said, eying Lang.

Ruthie rolled her eyes. "Don't be crude, Harley."

"Sorry to offend your delicate sensibilities, darlin'." He bowed to Ruthie. "Where's Chas tonight?"

"None of your beeswax," she said, and she stomped off to say hello to the Dillons.

"What's gotten into her?"

Maggie laughed, giving her boss a sharp look. "As if you didn't know."

"Hey, can't a man make an observation without gettin' his head bitten off?" Harley's face clouded as he looked at Beth. "Hey, Bethie, how you holdin' up? He's a shit and we're gonna—"

"Do nothing, thank you, Harl. I don't want to hear any more kill Bill jokes tonight, okay? I'd rather put the entire mess out of my mind for the next few hours. In fact, to that end, I think I'll have a margarita."

She headed for the bar, where a pitcher of frozen margaritas was already made, ready to pour. Raoul made her a drink and refrained from remarking about her situation, for which she was grateful. He was like a favorite uncle to Beth, and definitely her partner at the farm. His advice was solicited by organic farmers around the world. Ben had been encouraging him to create an interactive website and blog. So far, the stalwart farmer had resisted. *Maybe that would be a good project for me*, she thought, *to keep me extra busy?*

CHAPTER 6

"I'd love one of those if you're still pouring," a voice said to Raoul from behind Beth. "Lang Dillon. You probably don't remember me?" Lang extended his hand, which Raoul shook before turning back to the blender.

"Course I do. Nice to see you again, sir. Salt?"

"Absolutely."

"Here you go."

"Thanks." As they strolled across the terrace, Lang turned to Beth. "Glad to see you again so soon. You doing okay?"

She raised her glass. "This will help." His nearness was strangely comforting, even though she knew it was her vulnerable state calling the shots. That's all she needed. To fall for a man who would be racing out of town within the week.

"Uh-oh, already lapsing into alcoholism."

"Hardly. This'll put me under the table for the night since I've barely eaten all day."

"Then start now." He pointed to a tray of warm quesadillas Carmela had just set on the bar.

Beth shook her head.

"If you don't eat one of those before I count to three, I'm taking the drink."

Startled, she gazed into his sky-blue eyes. He was grinning, but his eyes were serious. Why did this stranger care whether she drank herself under the table? "Fine." She grabbed a triangular slice and took a big bite. Carmela's food was always to die for, and this was no exception. Warm cheese mingled with her special salsa and thin slices of avocado. An involuntary groan escaped before Beth could stifle it.

"That good, huh? I better try one." He did. "Oh, my God, that's the best quesadilla I've ever had."

She nodded and took another big bite. "Carmela is amazing."

"We don't get food like this out of Jon, I'll tell you that."

"I've had his cooking. It's fabulous."

"Too upscale California for my taste. This is the Southwest, after all."

He grabbed another slice of quesadilla and studied his companion. *Defeated* was the word that came to mind. Her sad eyes gazed out at the beautiful valley in front of them, thoughts a million miles away.

"Want a bite of this?"

Startled, she shook her head.

"Gonna be a magnificent sunset."

She nodded. "Almost always is."

Surprised at the depth of his feeling, Lang wanted to take the fragile, lovely creature standing next to him, fold her into his arms, and kiss away her terrible pain. What bastard had caused such misery?

"Beth?"

"Huh?" She turned away from the view to look up at him. His dazzling blue eyes took her breath away. As much as she had loved Bill, she honestly could not think of a time when he had taken her breath away.

"Would you have lunch with me tomorrow?"

"I can't. My sister-in-law Maggie and I are doing something. Do you remember her? Maggie Williams? She and my brother Ben married last year. That's their daughter." She pointed at Emma, who was wrestling with her grandfather and one of the ranch dogs.

"So, they've been together a while, then?"

She smiled. "On and off. It's a long story, for another time."

"She looks vaguely familiar. I should remember a beauty like her. She's positively radiant."

"She's four months pregnant."

"Ah, that's great for them."

"They renovated my grandparents' homestead. You can see it from the winery. Not too far from you guys, at the south end of Morgan's Run."

"I remember that place. We would ride up, hang out, have an occasional beer or two on the porch. Best view in the Valley."

"You should see it now. Ben and my brother Sam designed the restoration. It's twice its original size and, in my opinion, the most beautiful house in Saguaro, but don't tell either of our moms I said that."

"How 'bout dinner, then?"

"Excuse me?"

"If you're busy at lunch, have dinner with me tomorrow."

"Why?"

"'Cuz I asked?"

"I'm afraid I'm pretty pathetic company right now."

"Funny, I hadn't noticed."

Beth laughed.

"Ah, a smile. That's something. Have dinner with me, Beth. I don't bite, and you'll be helping me out big time."

"Oh?"

"I can only spend so much time with my parents without going stark raving mad."

"Well, if the situation is that desperate, I guess I'll have to have dinner with you."

"Great!" He gave her a smile that made Beth go weak in the knees, another thing that had never happened with steady, quiet Bill Sampson. At least Lang wasn't a cowboy. She had avoided cowboys her entire life, and she wasn't about to change her ways now.

"Come on, I'll introduce you or reacquaint you with some of the locals."

As they strolled toward Maggie, Harley, and Ben, Rose Dillon appeared on the terrace and waved at her brother.

"Hang on for a second," he said. "I'll be back soon."

As Beth rejoined her brother and the others, Lang greeted his sister with a huge bear hug. It had been over a year since the siblings had seen each other, when Rose was back east and had stopped off in Boston.

She wore cream-colored slacks and a white lacy sweater, her straight, shoulder-length ash-blond hair held back in a headband, hazel eyes dancing with light as she greeted her beloved sibling.

"Hey, Rosie!"

She smiled up, overjoyed to see him. "How you doing, big brother?"

"Well, I've survived an afternoon with the folks. Only ten days to go."

"Very funny. Can't you stay longer? I've missed you."

"Not if I want to retain an ounce of sanity. How's dad's drinking?" he whispered, pulling her aside.

"He has more than he should, but he's better than last year. The mini heart attack woke him up."

"Sorry to hear that your childhood sweetheart got married off to someone else," he said, eyeing Ben Morgan and his gorgeous wife from across the terrace. He knew only too well how his sister had pined away, year after year, crazy in love with the oldest Morgan son.

"Stop it. He's not my sweetheart, and I'm happy for him and Maggie."

"She's a looker, huh? Don't remember her."

"She's blossomed," Rose said, smiling at her brother. "How's your love life? Anyone new? Any word from Cilla?"

"Cilla's practically engaged to some boring billionaire, and I'm a lonely bachelor once again. How 'bout you?"

"No one serious. Ruthie persuaded me to try the online stuff."

"Oh, sis, no."

"It's kind of fun, actually. You learn a lot about yourself and meet some nice people."

"Really?"

"Yes. Besides, with my hours at the clinic, I have no time for socializing and meeting people." Rose worked at the Heavers Clinic, a pediatric surgical center in Tucson specializing in children's spinal injuries. She had helped found the clinic with her mentor, Christopher Heavers, but illness had necessitated that Heavers move back east. He was not expected to recover.

"So?"

"I've had a couple of dates with a lawyer from Tucson."

"And?"

"Later. We're being very rude. Let's join the party."

"Who's this Ruthie?

"Ruthie Morgan." Rose pointed to the youngest Morgan, who had now joined Emma and her dad in throwing balls for the dog.

"She's a real spitfire, that one. Saw her briefly at the farm this afternoon. She was practically a baby when I left."

"She's a sweetheart. She and Beth run the farm. They do a phenomenal job."

"Beth seems pretty phenomenal."

"Oh?" Rose turned to him, curious at the interest evident in his voice.

"Later, sis." He smiled as they walked over to join the others.

CHAPTER 7

Jaybo Dillon raised his glass to his fellow diners. "As usual, Carmela has outdone herself."

"Let's not forget Raoul," Ben Senior said. "He's our grill wizard. And where would this meal be without the fine wines from Saguaro Valley Winery?" He raised his glass, then turned first to Martha Dillon on his right, then Maggie on his left, clinking their glasses in toast.

They dined on grilled lamb from the farm and side dishes of chipotle mashed sweet potatoes, caramelized onions, glazed Hakurei turnips, and radish salsa. Carmela had also made a greens soufflé for Ben vegetarian, and her special miniburgers and sweet potato french fries for Emma. The wines, all selected to complement the meal, were crisp and delicious.

Cambridge and Boston had amazing restaurants, but Lang could not recall when he had had a better meal. Of course, it was also the company, seated as he was between Maggie and Beth, and across from Ben, Ruthie, and Harley. Rose sat next to her father, who sat at Leonora Morgan's left, and Emma was on her grandmother's right, reveling in every minute. Emma loved dinners at the big house. If she got bored, she would retreat to the kitchen with Carmela, but tonight, she sat watching and listening to the handsome stranger, who seemed very interested in her aunt Beth.

"He's a sly one," Harley whispered to Ruthie as he watched Lang converse with Beth and Maggie, both of them hanging on his every word.

"I think he's gorgeous," Ruthie whispered, smiling across the table at Lang.

Leonora Morgan hated to be left out of conversations happening at her dinner table. As she observed the pockets of hushed conversations, she decided action was needed. "So, Lang, darlin'. You're a sight for sore eyes. How long are we gonna get to keep you in Saguaro? I know I'd like to see lots more of you."

"Not long, I'm 'fraid. About ten days. Then I've got to head back. The business doesn't run on its own."

"Is it shut down this week, then?" Harley asked.

Surprised at the challenge in the cowboy's tone, he laughed. "Hardly. I have great employees, and it's an online business so I can do a lot from here." *What did he remember about Harley Langdon? Ben Morgan's buddy. Got all the girls. Cocky as hell?*

"Don't get your hands dirty typing on computers."

"Oh, Harley, you're such a dinosaur." Ruthie rolled her eyes and poked him.

"You're right," Lang replied, grinning. "But I find ways to get dirty. Love hiking, and I sell high-tech sporting equipment, so we're out all the time testing gear."

"Do you make riding gear?" Maggie asked.

"Not yet, but funny you should ask. We get a lot of calls for riding gear. In fact, we have designers workin' on this right now. Our company, Rambler Sports, sells other companies' products, but our best sellers are our own designs. We're hoping the riding equipment will be a new niche for us. I'd love to pick your brain while I'm here. Come down to the stables, see what you're using, hear about your needs."

"Anytime," Ben said, forestalling what he feared might be a less than welcoming remark from his partner. What was Harley's beef with Dillon, anyway? Seemed like a nice enough guy, and at least he was distracting Beth from her heartache.

Ruthie gave Lang her sweetest smile. "We'd would love to have you come out to the farm, wouldn't we, Bethie?"

"Of course," Beth said.

Deer in the headlights, Lang thought, watching Beth. *She's drifted off again.* Impulsively, he reached under the tablecloth and took her hand. He was surprised when, instead of withdrawing, she wrapped her slender fingers around his and held on.

Like the rest of her body, Beth's hand was icy cold. Lang's warmth coursed through her like a heat wave, and she almost cried with gratitude at his gesture of kindness. The rest of the table remained oblivious to the hand-holding, except for both Bens. Father and son had been watching daughter and sister when Lang's hand disappeared under the table. The change in Beth's demeanor surprised them. She seemed to relax rather than stiffen. While they were both glad for the comfort Lang seemed to bring her, each in his own way, feared for her vulnerable heart. Lang Dillon would be leaving town in less than two weeks, and neither father nor son wished to see a broken heart left behind.

As Carmela served dessert—her specialty, a caramel flan—the talk turned to the upcoming Valley Fair in two weeks. One of Arizona's largest, most popular county fairs, it drew people from hundreds of miles away. Many of the ranch's animals were shown. The wranglers and the young riders who took lessons from Maggie and her assistant, Jeb Barnes, were out in full regalia. It was the Valley's biggest event of the year.

"Lang, you can't leave before the fair," Ruthie said.

Leonora frowned at her youngest. "Ruthie, please don't wave your spoon around with food on it. She's right, though, Lang, darlin'. What's a couple more days? It's the weekend after next."

"Not sure, Mrs. Morgan. Lot of stuff waiting for me at home."

"Call me Leonora, please!"

"Nora, leave the boy alone," Ben Senior said, smiling at his wife.

Beth listened, wondering whether some of what was waiting at home was a girlfriend, fiancée, or significant other. Slowly, sadly, she withdrew her hand and picked up her dessert spoon. As if sensing the change in their interaction, Lang moved closer, his thigh resting against hers. She did not move away.

Later, as the Dillons said goodnight to their hosts, Lang found Beth in the kitchen. "Hey, wanted to say goodnight. Pick you up at seven tomorrow night?"

"I don't know, Lang. I'm not, you're not…" She was sputtering, groping for what she wanted to say. Every fiber of her being longed to go out with him, to lose herself in his arms, in his kiss, in his sky-blue eyes. But at the same time, warning bells clanged. *He's leaving. He's trouble. He's probably engaged back home. Don't get any closer.*

"It's dinner, Beth. Not a marriage proposal. Just a friendly dinner. I don't know many people in the Valley, and I would like to think we could be friends, okay?"

"Fine. See you at seven."

"Good night, then." He leaned forward and kissed her cheek, leaving hot, searing fire in his wake. At that moment, Carmela appeared with a tray of dishes and found Beth blushing crimson as the handsome Dillon son made his exit. The wise cook smiled and said a silent prayer for the two, who were, in her opinion, made for each other.

CHAPTER 8

"I'd be careful, Lang," his sister said as they sat sipping tea on their parents' front porch. "She's pretty fragile right now."

"I know. I'm trying to cheer her up."

"Well, just be careful. For your own sake and hers. I've never seen Beth Morgan unglued the way she is now. She's always been the stalwart, steady presence in that wild group. She was their rock during Emma's long rehabilitation."

"I heard about that. Pretty remarkable."

"Yes, it was. Chris was sure we could help her, and he was right."

"How's Doc Heavers doin', anyway?"

"Actually, a bit better. We're hoping for a miracle there, too."

"Hope so."

"I cannot imagine a world where I cannot seek his wisdom and advice."

"So, Ben Morgan fathered a child he didn't know about for four years?"

Rose nodded, her eyes sad. "He's over the moon about her. Making up for lost time, I expect."

"You're not over him any more than I am Cilla."

"Yes, I am. Stop it. Are you still regretting the breakup with Cilla?"

"No, we weren't good for each other, and we would have driven each other crazy. It's just…there are things about her I miss."

"Of course there are. I liked Cilla."

"Don't bullshit me, sis. You were thrilled to see the back of her."

"Was not!"

"Was, too. Now, tell me about Dad," he said, lowering his voice.

"Don't worry about whispering. He sleeps like a log, and Mom has a white noise machine. He sleeps in his old study most nights. Says it's very British of them to sleep in separate bedrooms, but it's really because he snores like a freight train and often drinks and smokes cigars at night."

"Lucky Mom."

"I'm not home that often, but it seems like he might be doing a little better. I'm a bit worried about the anniversary party next weekend. It's those kinds of events when he tends to overdo, and then there's an incident."

"Like?"

"Now, don't get in a rage if I tell you this."

"Out with it, Rosie."

"As you know, he often yells at Mom when he's drunk, but a couple of months ago after an event at the club, don't remember what, Mom was trying to calm him down and get him to bed and he lashed out and hit her. Broke her jaw."

"Jesus Christ, why didn't you call me?"

"She tried to pretend she'd fallen, but Neecy called me. I came right away and took her to an emergency room in Tucson because she refused to go to Valley Hospital. While we waited for the doctor, I wormed it out of her. She was so embarrassed. Didn't go out of the house for over a month. Had to cancel everything, all her Cowbelle work, Women's Union, bridge. Leonora Morgan called constantly, wanting to come over, and finally just showed up. Mom confided in her, I guess, but swore her to secrecy."

"Will she respect that?"

Rose nodded. "Leonora has her faults, but she's Mom's best friend and would do anything for her. She wanted to talk to Dad or have Ben Senior do it, but Mom forbade it."

"Rosie, you should have called. Has this happened before?"

"Mom swears no, if you can believe it. Says this time was an accident."

"Did you talk to Dad?"

"Yes, but he stalked out of the room and told me it was none of my business."

"Why the hell are we throwing that bastard a party?"

"It's for Mom, Lang. She deserves to celebrate a little."

"Celebrate what? She's been saddled with that asshole for forty years. The party should be celebrating her leaving him, or better still, kicking him out. It was her inheritance that made all this possible. She has good help. They could run this without that bastard."

Rose reached over and put her hand on her brother's. "That's Mom's decision. We need to stay out of it, at least for now."

"If he so much as raises his voice to her, I'm going to knock him silly."

"Let's go to bed. You've got a busy day ahead of you, I hear. Maybe when you take the farm tour, I'll come along."

"Oh? Of course, you'd be welcome."

Rose laughed. "Now who's bullshitting? Besides, Mom's list is a mile long. I've got to get started on it, and I'm giving some items to you."

"Well, then, why don't we both tour the farm, then do errands together?"

She patted his hand again. "No, thanks. I've seen it. It's amazing, though, so you should go while you're here. Mom and I are going shopping for last-minute party stuff and maybe some clothes before I start on the party list."

"Lucky you. Night, sis. Good to see you." He kissed the top of her head. Then they headed into the house together.

CHAPTER 9

Beth woke feeling disoriented, expecting to find herself in her own bed at the condo, not in her brother's old bedroom. When she occasionally spent the night at the ranch, she usually slept on the couch in the farm office. She realized that it had been at least six years since she had slept at the big house.

It was a pleasant, peaceful room. Even though the cowboys of their youth still galloped across the faded wallpaper, their mother had a wonderful eye for color and worked hard to make sure her guests were comfortable. Beth pulled back the quilt and rose, grateful that her cell phone was broken. As if on cue, the silly thing rang. It was still sitting in the corner, where she had thrown it. The plastic protector was off, battery half out, and the thing was actually ringing!

She padded over and saw "Bill" on the cracked display window. She considered flushing it down the toilet, but picked it up and came back to sit on the side of the bed. "Hello?"

"Oh, Beth, thank God. I've been so worried."

"You didn't look worried the last time I saw you."

"Please, let me explain."

"No, I don't want to hear it, Bill. How could you? You brought Skyler to our home. "

"Listen, sweetheart. Please let me explain. I want to see you. It's not what you think."

"Please don't call me that ever again. I don't want to see you. I'm staying at the ranch until I decide where I want to live."

"Beth, please come home so we can talk."

"That is no longer my home. Do you think I could ever sleep in that bed after what I saw yesterday?"

"Oh, God, Beth, I'm so sorry. I would never choose to hurt you. Not in a million years."

"I've gotta go."

"No, wait!"

"Bill, I'm hanging up now. Please don't keep calling. My cell phone's in pieces and I'm not sure how long it'll work. Calling the house phone won't do you any good, either, since you're not the most popular person in this house right now."

"Oh, God. Does your whole family know?"

"Not yet. Just Mom, Dad, Ruthie, and Ben and Maggie, but they'll all know after this weekend when they come for the Dillons' party."

"They must hate me. I guess I'm no longer invited to that party."

When had Bill become so narcissistic? she wondered. Already he had made it all about him. "Bill, I really can't talk about this now. In a few weeks, when I've figured things out, I'll be in touch."

"A few weeks? Beth, please, I need to talk now! To make things right!"

"Things will never be right."

"Please, Beth!"

"I'm late. I've gotta go."

"Where are you going? Work?"

"Where I go is no longer your business. Goodbye, Bill." She hung up the phone.

She found her sister just finishing breakfast. "Hey, Ruthie, are you sure about my taking the morning off? Isn't gonna drive you crazy after yesterday?"

"Absolutely not. Take the whole day if you want. We're fine."

"No, I've got a rep coming in at one, from San Diego Markets. I'll try to get there by noon. Lang is stopping by sometime for a tour, too."

"Oh, boy! I hope he comes this morning while you're gone."

"Around two, I believe."

"What's the fun in that? When you're around, he only has eyes for you."

"No, he doesn't. He's just being friendly. Probably feels sorry for me."

"Baloney."

Beth laughed, swatting her sister. "See you later."

CHAPTER 10

"I think while you're with Beth, I'll drive into Tucson and kill Bill Sampson," Ben said, kissing the back of his wife's neck, nuzzling, as his hands reached round and stroked her belly. Still newlyweds, they fell more in love each day.

Maggie stood at their new kitchen sink, the window above it affording a spectacular view of the Valley. "You will do no such thing. Leave it alone, Ben. I mean it. Bill's not a bad guy, just weak and stupid."

"And a bastard," he whispered, knowing Emma was in the next room.

"That, too. Poor Beth. I thought they'd be together for the long haul."

"Not me. Always thought he was a slippery customer."

"No, you didn't."

"Then why were they together for ten years and he still hadn't proposed?"

"Maybe he did and Beth wasn't ready? No one can say what goes on in relationships behind closed doors."

"Hmm. I'd still like to kill him, and I'm sure between Harley, Robbie, Sam, and Kyle, we could get a great posse together and string him up."

"Do your brothers know yet?"

"Not unless Ruthie or my parents called them. But all three'll be here for the Dillons' party."

"Which Bill was invited to."

"And won't be coming."

"Well, I'm off. Dad should be here for Emma soon. Are you sure you're okay waiting for him?"

"Absolutely. Have fun, sweetie." He gave her a long, lingering kiss and an affectionate pat on her bottom as she grabbed her purse and headed out.

"Love you both!" she called and headed to the truck.

Fifteen minutes later, the two women were seated in a back booth at Gracie's Diner in the center of town. "What can I get you, ladies?" Stacy, the waitress smiled down at them, pouring coffee for Beth and setting down Maggie's pot of tea.

They each ordered the omelet special, and Stacy headed off. "Is she still dating Jeb?" Beth asked, watching the redhead disappear through the kitchen doors.

"Far as I know."

"Did they go to school together?"

"There's a couple of years' age difference," Maggie said. "And I think Stacy grew up in Yuma. Dad runs the rodeo every year."

"They'd be cute together. I love Jeb. Such a cutie."

"That he is, and he knows it, too." Maggie gazed at her sister-in-law, eyes filled with warmth.

"How you holdin' up?"

"Well, my day started with a phone call from Bill on my cell that was broken in pieces on the floor."

"Oh, Beth, how was that?"

"Horrible. He wants to see me, but I told him to stay away."

Maggie nodded. "When you're stronger. When you're ready."

"Oh, God, Maggie, what am I going to do? My whole life was Bill. I mean, I have the farm and I love my work and my family, but everything else was him. I left the Valley on purpose. To have a life beyond the ranch, and we did."

"And you will again, if that's what you want."

"But it was all him, all his friends. My entire social life is gone if I don't stay with him."

"Are you considering that?"

"No…maybe. I don't know. It's just I feel so numb and empty without him. Knowing I won't be going home to cooking dinner together and share stories of our days. Even when he's away, we always talk at night, sometimes for hours. Bill's the only person I've ever been able to do that with."

Stacy appeared with the omelets, asked if they needed anything else, and quickly departed.

Beth looked down at her food and felt sick. She tried to take a bite and the food almost choked her. "I had no sleep last night, except for about fifteen minutes just before sunrise. I don't do well with no sleep."

Maggie reached over and squeezed her hand. "Give it a couple of days. If it doesn't get better, I'm sure the doctor can prescribe a mild sleep medication."

"And before you know it, I'll have lapsed into drug addiction and alcoholism."

"No, you won't, but you're in shock. You need sleep to recover."

"Would you take him back?"

"Oh, Beth, you're the only one who can answer that. When you're feeling stronger, maybe you can talk and see how you feel? People certainly do work through things like this and stay together."

Beth stared at her sister-in-law for a moment. "We've never talked like this, have we?"

Maggie smiled. "Thank goodness, we've never needed to."

"No, I mean close, about personal things."

"No, I guess not."

"I'm sorry, Maggie."

"For what?"

"For all the years you struggled to raise Emma alone."

"I wasn't alone. My dad's been with me every step of the way."

"Yes, but you could have used a friend. Here we've been working together all these years and I never once asked you to go for coffee, or a meal. Never reached out and asked if you could use help or anything."

"Beth, you've been an amazing friend. Look what you and all your siblings did for Emma."

"But that was only because my knucklehead brother came to his senses and our parents woke up and corralled us together. I'm talking about before."

"Well, I would put that off your list of worries at the moment. The farm and stables are separate operations, and we rarely bump into each other. And since Emma's birth, I haven't been the most approachable person, if truth be told. I kept to myself for self-protection. Rarely let anyone near me. Look what your poor brother went through, trying to get to know me."

They laughed, and each took a bite of a delicious omelet filled with vegetables and oozing with Gruyère cheese, an artisan brand produced locally. Beth's included farm-cured bacon; Maggie's did not. Gracie bought almost all of her ingredients from the Valley. The bacon and eggs came from the farm at Morgan's Run, as did the vegetables. The second bite was a little easier to swallow, and Beth forced herself to take a third, then a fourth.

By the time Maggie pulled up at the big house, Beth felt calmer, warmed by the breakfast and her sister-in-law's company.

"Thanks, Mags."

"Anytime."

"You headed home?"

"No, I've got work clothes in the back of the truck. Lessons all afternoon."

"Well, thanks again."

"My pleasure. I'll check in later, okay?"

Beth smiled and Maggie reached over to take her hand. "You know, in a way, we're a lot alike. I've never had many women friends, just Dara. Friends?"

"Friends," Beth said, squeezing her hand. "Have a great afternoon with the kiddies."

Chapter 11

The rep from San Diego Markets was waiting when she arrived at the farm office shortly before one. Beth had intended to arrive at noon, but her mother had waylaid her as she changed for work. The farm shipped most of their produce east, but the San Diego Markets had been one of their first customers many years earlier, and they remained loyal.

When she walked Rich Myers to his car an hour later, Beth realized the time with him had been a welcome respite. They'd talked organics and shipments, and she had not had a minute to think about the heartache. *Work. I will immerse myself in work until I can figure out what the hell to do with the tattered remains of my life.* She headed for the washing barn to pick up a golf cart.

She decided to start Lang's tour with a ride out to the edge of the gardens, then swing over to the west meadows, where sheep and cattle grazed. Then they would come back via the pastures where pigs and chicken ran free. After that, she would park the cart and they could walk through the processing barns, if he was interested.

No sooner had she pulled up to the office with the cart than she spied the now familiar beige Rover driving up the dirt road. He waved and parked alongside her truck. "Hey, this is amazing!"

"Thanks. It's taken several hardworking generations of Morgans to get to this point."

Beth was so glad to see him, she almost fainted. Just being around him made her feel warm, safe, and almost whole. She knew he would be gone in less than two weeks, but it was sure nice to have him now, another respite from the emptiness that stretched in front of her.

What was she going to do? She could not live with her parents forever, or even for a few weeks. As she watched Lang approach, she remembered that the senior Morgans were about to embark on a two-month cruise. If she could make it until they departed in three weeks, she would be fine hanging out with Ruthie and Carmela for a while.

As she waved, giving him a wan smile, Lang noted the dark circles ringing her lovely hazel eyes. Not a wink of sleep last night, he guessed. He'd had more than a few of those nights after Cilla left. He could still hear her words that last day: *It's your house, your money, and your insensitivity, and I want nothing more to do with them or you.*

"I thought we'd start by taking a ride out to the edge of the gardens," Beth said. "That way, you can get an idea of the scope."

"Perfect. You driving?"

"Hop in."

As he sat down, his thigh grazed hers, and Lang reached over and took her hand. "Thanks for taking time out of your day for this. I'm really interested in what you're doing out here."

She averted her eyes. "My pleasure. Anything to distract me from the rest of the mess. I mean, that didn't come out right. What I meant to say is, I'm happy to do it."

He reached over and cupped her chin, turning her so their eyes met. "Beth, don't feel like you have to be brave for me. I went through a breakup of a long-time relationship last year. It sucks. Better to let it out. Cry when you need to and lean on your friends."

Tears rimmed her eyes as she regarded him sadly. "I'm not very good at leaning on people."

"Well, then, maybe it's time to start. Let's see what this operation's all about, shall we?"

He smiled his drop-dead, killer smile. She turned to start the cart, afraid that if she didn't, she would throw herself into his arms and beg him to take her away from all this. *Friends*, she told herself. *Just friends.*

They spent a happy hour riding from one end of the farm to the other, stopping to watch the animals, talking to some of the workers, and enjoying the incredible views up and down the Valley. An orographic effect, of cloud formation and with it lots of moisture had created this green space, surrounded by mountains with desert beyond to the east, west, north, and south. Aside from six enormous ranches that included Morgan's Run and the Dillons' winery, a largely undiscovered town existed. Saguaro Valley was an oasis for its roughly three thousand year-round residents and an equal number of snowbirds, tourists, and wealthy vacationers who found their way through the passes in at various points in the year. The Morgans, the Dillons, and a few others like them were responsible for the undiscovered part. They zealously guarded the Valley from outsiders and had bought up most of the land, deeding it back to conservancy groups with the understanding that they could farm it, but that it could never be developed.

As they parked at the largest washing barn, Raoul emerged. "Hey, Beth, can I talk to you a sec?"

The three headed into the barn. The older man had skin the color of burnt leather, and his coal-black eyes shone with warmth. He wore faded black jeans with a tear in one thigh, a faded green farm tee shirt, and a wide-brimmed straw Stetson, stained with mud and grease.

"Enos is coming Wednesday. Do we have enough people or do you want me to call into town?"

While Beth and Ruthie technically ran the farm, Raoul managed all the livestock and ran most decisions by Beth. It was an interesting partnership, since he had trained both sisters from the time they showed interest in the farm. The relationship worked because of the deep mutual respect they had for one another. Neither Beth nor her sister interfered with Raoul's decisions, and he supported their quiet, generous leadership. The days they collaborated most closely were slaughtering and market days.

Enos Walker was the person who slaughtered all their animals, except the chickens, which Raoul did himself with a cone-shaped contraption that made the deaths humane, quick, and stress-free for the animals. Enos had a variety of techniques that he used to slaughter each animal, each breed, as humanely as possible. An expert marksman, he shot the steers as they grazed; they died instantly in the place they had spent their entire lives. The pigs, lambs, and sheep were slaughtered in the slaughtering barn, but with as little stress to the animals as they could manage.

"How many?"

"Two steers, eight pigs, and a dozen lambs."

"Better get a couple of the local kids. You'll need help bringing the beef in."

"Will do. Nice to see you, Mr. Dillon."

"Lang, please."

Raoul tipped his hat and disappeared as they stepped back into the sunlight.

"So you slaughter everything here. That's unusual, isn't it?"

"Not for farms where they care about their animals. If we're gonna eat or make a profit from their sacrificed lives, we're sure as hell gonna see that they don't die in fear and stress. Enos and Raoul are incredible. I've never seen an animal scared in their presence. We've consulted a lot of people about this. Temple Grandin's work has helped enormously. Do you know of Temple's work?"

He shook his head.

"She's a professor of animal science at Colorado State. She's also an autistic activist. She's spent the better part of her life consulting to the livestock industry on animal behavior and humane ways of keeping and killing livestock. She visited Morgan's Run five years ago. It was such an honor to have her. We had already implemented most of the slaughtering practices we use today. She was really impressed."

"Is there anything you can't do, Beth Morgan, farmer and livestock breeder extraordinaire?"

"Plenty, like keeping the coyotes away from our lambs. We're getting donkeys and a couple of herding dogs. We'll see how that works out. Would you like to see the other barns?"

"Love to, unless I'm keeping you from your work."

She laughed. "We're a well-oiled machine here. Can't you tell?"

"It's really good to hear you laugh, Beth. I'll have to dredge up all the ridiculous jokes I know so I can hear that beautiful sound again."

As he spoke, he felt her stiffen beside him. When he turned, her face was ashen as she stared straight ahead. He followed her gaze and saw a stranger emerging from the farm office.

"Beth, hi." Bill waved as he approached, gaze moving from her to the handsome stranger beside her. *Who the hell was this cowboy?*

She said nothing but stood stiff and silent beside Lang. When Bill reached them, she said, "Lang Dillon, this is Bill Sampson. Bill was just leaving."

"Beth, please? Could you excuse us, Mr. Dillon?"

"No, he could not. I told you not to come."

"The lady doesn't want to see you right now, pal."

"I'm not your pal, so piss off."

"Like hell I will!"

Beth threw out her arms. "That's enough. Wait here, Bill."

She grabbed Lang's arm and pulled him toward the Rover.

"Don't do this, Beth. I can get rid of him in two seconds flat."

As they stood at the far side of the Rover, she placed her hand on his strong forearm. "Thank you, but Bill is my problem. I truly didn't want to see him, but now that he's here, I'll give him a few minutes."

"Bad idea." Without thinking, he placed his hands on the curve of her hips, wanting nothing more than to pull her close for a lingering kiss. That would give the sniveling bastard something to think about.

"Probably, but I might as well get it over with." She placed her hands on his strong shoulders, longing to run them along his chiseled jaw. "You go. I'll see you tonight. Still picking me up at seven?"

"Wouldn't miss it. Are you sure? I can stay. I'll just sit in my car until he leaves."

She laughed. "I'll be fine. We'll talk in the office. Fear not. If I get into trouble, Ruthie or Raoul will come to my rescue."

He leaned forward and kissed her forehead. "Until tonight."

"Yes," she answered, breathless at his nearness. She waved as he pulled out of the drive, then turned to face Bill, who had watched the entire scene slack-jawed.

CHAPTER 12

"Didn't take *you* long, did it? Who the hell was that cowboy?"

"He's not a cowboy, Bill. He's from Boston. Come on. We can talk in the office."

Somehow, Lang's kiss had emboldened her, given her strength and courage to face the man who had broken her heart so completely.

Once the office door had closed, Beth sat in her swivel chair and indicated one of two metal chairs for him. "I only have a few minutes, and really don't have anything to say to you right now. But since you've barged in, say what's on your mind so I can get back to work."

"Or run after your new boyfriend."

The man sitting across from her didn't even sound like her Bill. "Can we please get on with this?"

"Aren't you even going to tell me who he is?"

"Is this really why you drove all the way from Tucson? To check up and see if I'd gotten a new boyfriend yet? I haven't, though it's none of your business. Lang Dillon is a friend. Now, what do you want?"

"I want you back, of course."

"Well, that's not happening anytime soon. How long have you and Skyler been screwing?"

"Is that relevant?"

"What do you think?"

"It's over. Totally over."

"How long?"

"About a year."

Beth reeled back as if she had been kicked in the chest. "A year? I expected you to say a few weeks or months."

"Beth, it doesn't matter. She doesn't matter. She means nothing to me. I love you."

"Oh, that's flattering. You've been having a year-long affair that means nothing. Now, you're willing to just drop your lover like a hot potato in order to keep your comfy life going."

"That's not how it is, not at all."

Beth stared at him. She felt nothing. A numbness crept over her as she gazed at the man she had loved since she was eighteen. Bill was good-looking. Tall, thin, with sandy hair, he looked like the academic he was. His was the wiry build of a hiker and rock climber. She had loved their hiking trips but had never shared his passion for rock climbing. She had tried it a few times, then encouraged him to go alone. It was on the tip of her tongue to ask if Skyler was a rock climber, but she stayed silent. It was none of her business, and she didn't want to know about their relationship.

"Bill, it's over. I can't see any way around it. I could never be with you again. The image of you and her, in our bed, will never go away."

"Oh, Beth, please." He hopped off his chair and knelt in front of her, hugging her round the knees.

Horrified, she tried to stand, but he held on to her. "Bill, let go, now." When she gazed down, she saw he had tears in his eyes. "Look, why don't we give each other a couple of weeks, then get together when things aren't so raw."

"I'm afraid if we wait, I'll lose you."

You've already lost me, she thought sadly as she extracted herself from his grasp and moved toward the door. "I'm sorry, but I've got work to do."

"Where is he?"

Beth heard her brother's voice outside the door and cringed. *Just what I need.* She raised a finger to Bill. "Stay here. I'll be right back."

"No, I'll go. I'm not afraid of Ben Morgan."

Bill stood, pushed by, and reached for the door handle. "Have fun with your new boyfriend." His voice was cold and cutting. It was a voice Beth had never heard Bill use before.

She followed him out to find her brother standing by Bill's car.

"Please step aside, Morgan. I'm leaving."

"Yeah, like that's gonna happen."

"Ben, leave him be! There's nothing for you to do here."

Ben stepped aside and Bill slipped into his car. "I'm doing this for her sake, not yours. If it were up to me, you'd be pounded into the ground. You're an asshole, Sampson. Don't you dare come here again unless my sister invites you."

Bill stared straight ahead as he started the car. Without a word, he drove away.

Ben came to her side. "You okay?"

"Yes, oh savior of mine. And for the record, I was handling it."

"Well, just wanted you to know I had your back."

"I know."

"I hear you're having dinner with Lang Dillon. Is that wise?"

"He's a friend and, to tell the truth, a welcome distraction right now."

"Well, be careful, Beth. That's all I'm saying."

"Thanks, big brother," she said, hugging him. "I'll be fine."

CHAPTER 13

Lang pulled up promptly at seven. Beth had forbade her parents from coming out, and she met him on the porch. She was wearing one of her few dresses and the only one she had grabbed in her escape from the condo. She would have to go shopping before the Dillons' party, or slip into to the condo when she knew Bill would be at work. Although she detested shopping, she decided that in this case, it was the lesser of two evils. There were a few decent clothing stores in Saguaro, mostly catering to wealthy ranch owners and the tourists who frequented the ranches and the spa on Rogue Mountain.

Beth nearly swooned when he stepped from the Rover. He was dressed casually in dark slacks, a blue dress shirt, and a gray cashmere sweater. How had she never noticed growing up how incredibly sexy and handsome Lang Dillon was? Her body trembled as she walked down the steps toward him.

Lang watched her shy approach, equally stunned. Her pale green sleeveless dress hugged her subtle curves. The bodice caressed her round, small breasts, while the skirt flared out and swished in the slight evening breeze. A soft white shawl was draped over her shoulders. Lovely did not begin to describe the self-conscious creature standing three feet away from him.

"Wow, Beth, you look sensational!"

She blushed. "Thanks. You don't look so bad yourself."

He held the door and she slipped into the car, leaving the scent of gardenias and some other exotic fragrance. *Intoxicating.*

He had made reservations at the Red Mesa Inn. Nestled in the foothills, ten miles from the nearest home or business, it was a popular honeymoon spot for those desiring seclusion and privacy. The inn's terrace bistro was one of a handful of five-star restaurants in the southwest. At Rose's suggestion, Lang had booked them a corner table with a spectacular view of the mountains.

As they were ushered to their seats, he was just making a mental note to thank his sister when he glanced over at Beth. Her face was ashen and her hands trembled.

"Beth, what's wrong?"

"Ghosts, that's all," she said, shaking herself as the maitre d' seated her.

"Would you rather have another table, sir?" the man asked.

"We're fine, thanks," Lang said, his tone making it clear that the maitre d' should disappear, which he did.

Lang sat and reached across to take her hands. "Talk to me."

"It's fine, really. Just a surprise."

"We can go to the Shake and Burger on Gila if you don't want to be here. What is it?"

"Bill brought me here on my birthday last year. We sat at this very table."

"I'll ask them to change us. There were empty tables inside."

"No, don't be silly." Tears rimmed her hazel eyes, and she dabbed at them with her napkin. "I'm okay, really."

"Come on." He stood and held out his hand. Hand in hand, they headed inside. When he spied the maitre d', he asked Beth to wait a short distance away.

When he returned, he announced, "All set. Do you want to stay here and find a table with a different perspective? There are several, or we can find another place to eat."

"Well, I do love the food here."

Lang nodded to the maitre d' and turned to her. "Ready?"

She smiled, and they were ushered out to a private terrace with one table, located inside the inn's walled garden. Flowers bloomed everywhere—in beds, climbing the stone walls, and in colorful ceramic pots. When the maitre d' vanished, Lang asked, "Is this okay?"

"Okay? Lang, this must have cost you a fortune! I never knew this garden existed."

"According to Oscar, with whom I've gotten very close, it's usually reserved for honeymooners or people like that."

"It's beautiful. Reminds me of one of my favorite childhood books, *The Secret Garden*."

"After it had been restored."

She looked at him in surprise.

"What? You don't think boys liked that book? Loved it. My mom read it aloud to Rosie and me several times."

She laughed. "A man of hidden depths. If I forget later, thank you. This is such a special night for me."

"Seems like you needed something special after your afternoon. Did it go okay with your…not sure what to call him. Partner? Maybe ex, maybe not?"

"Bill. You can call him Bill. It was fine and relatively brief. Exit was a bit rocky. My big brother rushed in to defend me and intimidate Bill."

"Good for him."

She shrugged. "Maybe we could have a moratorium on that subject for tonight? Tell me about your work, your company, and life in the big city."

"Not much to tell. Started Rambler Sports eight years ago, and we've done really well. My partner, Bertie—Roberta—is the business whiz, and I've handled sales and promotion. Bertie and her wife, Joan, handle all the daily retail oversight, and we have a couple of warehouses that ship for us. I'm lucky. It's a great group of people. It's actually fun to go to work. My job is either online or out in the field. I have a bunch of sales calls to make as I head east. May take a couple of day trips to Tucson and Flagstaff while I'm here."

Throughout a spectacular seven-course meal, Lang regaled her with stories of Boston and his experiences since leaving Saguaro. As they sipped cappuccino and brandy, she asked, "What happened with your relationship, if you don't mind my asking? If I'm prying, you don't have to tell me."

"We grew apart. That simple."

"Oh." Her lovely eyes gazed at him, clearly wanting more, as if his story might somehow help her survive her current nightmare.

"Cilla and I went to Middlebury together. We both hiked, skied. Seemed to have all kinds of common ground. Then we moved to Boston and things changed. She suddenly hated the outdoors and got back into the social scene. She grew up on Beacon Hill and was thrilled to be back, hanging out with her debutante crowd. The whole scene drove me right up the wall. We started doing more and more things without each other. I'd go hiking, she'd party, and then we meet up somewhere in between."

"Sounds a little like Bill and me, actually. I mean, I'm outdoorsy, but he's a rock climber, and I don't like it."

"My business has me outdoors a lot. Only tried rock climbing once, with a client, and didn't much like it. Too hairy."

"What worked with you and Cilla? I mean, what were the in-between times like? Were there any things you liked to do together?"

"Well, aside from the obvious...." He blushed. "We both liked hanging around on Sundays, the whole paper thing, long breakfasts. We liked walking in the city, theater, music, getting lost in the Fine Arts Museum on a rainy afternoon."

"Sounds like fun."

"It was, and in truth, I miss it. But the in-between times became fewer and scarcer, and we started quarreling more. She would be pissed that I wouldn't go to a party or another boring dinner with people I didn't know and she barely did. It was time."

"Was the decision mutual?"

"I brought it up, but yes, in the end it was mutual. Basically, she had another boyfriend our last year together. A hedge fund guy who was only too happy to be her social escort. They're practically engaged now."

"Were they...?"

"Having an affair? I don't know. He mostly took her to all the parties I refused to attend. Truth was, by the time we broke up, I didn't care what they were doing. That's how I knew it was time."

"But you miss her?"

"Sometimes. We were together a long time, but I wouldn't go back. What I miss isn't there anymore."

Beth looked down at her hands. Her long, slender fingers toyed with her empty brandy glass.

"Want another?"

"No, thanks. Not unless you'd like to carry me out."

He laughed. "Would be my pleasure. Sorry if I talked about myself all night."

"Don't be. It was just what I needed to get out of my head and forget for a few hours what a mess my life is."

Her long, dark hair was down, straight, fine wisps caressing her shoulders. Errant strands fell across her face and he reached over and smoothed them back behind one ear, his touch soft and gentle. "Ready to go, then?"

She nodded. "But I do hate to leave this beautiful place."

"Then we'll come again. Let's make a pact that the next time I'm in Saguaro, we'll have dinner here, in this very spot."

"That'll be when? In a decade or so? Could be under new ownership and have turned into a Marriott by then."

Before he could respond, the waiter brought the check, which Lang insisted upon paying. As they made their way out, Oscar the maitre d' gave him a wink and a smile. She suspected that Oscar and the Red Mesa Inn had been well compensated for their special dinner.

Lang held the door again as she alighted at the house. There was a full moon, and the sky was bright, with stars casting a warm glow over the Valley. "It's so light here," he said. "The stars are incredible."

"Feel like a walk? There's a pretty one to the creek."

"What about the wildlife, rattlesnakes, you know?"

"We have a good supply of anti-venom."

"Why do I not find that comforting? Yet another reason why I left the Valley."

"We'll be fine. Let me grab a backpack from the shed, just in case."

CHAPTER 14

It was a warm spring night, but the breeze had kicked up. Beth left her shawl on the porch and grabbed an old sweatshirt from the shed. "Sorry, practicality won out," she said, when she returned.

"Very becoming." *You haven't any idea how lovely you are, Beth Morgan. You'd look sensational in a burlap sack.*

"Shall we?"

The soft dirt path was narrow in spots. They continually bumped shoulders and their arms grazed one another as they proceeded. Each time, his touch sent ripples of warmth through her. She longed to take his hand but dared not. *Protect yourself. He's leaving soon and your heart is fragile and broken. Don't lose it again so soon.*

Fireflies flickered and flitted in the brush and field grasses on either side. "I love this walk. At this time of year, with the lightning bugs, it feels as if the stars have come down from the sky and are dancing around us."

"It's incredible."

"Here we are," she said softly. "Unless you're up for wading or swimming, this is the end of this path."

The creek meandered slowly before them, stars reflected in its dark, swirling depths. It was on the tip of his tongue to suggest skinny-dipping, but he wasn't sure he wanted to meet a copperhead on his way out. Instead, he turned and gazed down at her, and their eyes met in the rosy moonlight. Without thinking, he kissed her. Not a quick, friendly kiss. His lips parted hers and delved deep, drawing her to him. Amazed at her response, which matched his own feelings, he began slowly caressing her back, hands moving up and around to cup her soft, round breasts.

Beth moaned, instantly lost in a haze of desire and longing. Before she knew it, his kisses trailed down her neck, nuzzling as he unbuttoned her dress, kissing her soft skin, journeying to circle and tease her nipples through her thin, lacy bra.

As she reached up, arms circling his neck, Beth returned his kisses as she felt him grow hard against her. With a boldness that took her breath away, she moved one hand down to caress his manhood, breathless at his size.

"Oh, Jesus, Beth, you're killing me. Tell me to stop now, or I'm not sure I can."

"Please don't stop," she whispered.

He reached under her skirt and slipped her panties off, fingers caressing and probing, slick with her wetness. She was ready for him, so ready, like no woman Lang had ever been with. He reached round and cupped her buttocks, lifted her, and wrapped her legs around him. Huskily he whispered in her ear, kissing and teasing the soft lobe, "this is as far as I go, darlin', without whipping the old condom out."

Beth reached down and unzipped him, fingers slipping in to release him. "What are you waiting for?" she murmured.

He reached back and grabbed his wallet, slipping out the condom he kept there for emergencies. "Old condom" was not far from the truth. He prayed it was still useable. He had not planned on this tonight, that was for sure. With hand and teeth, he ripped open the small packet and was sheathed in ten seconds, all the while kissing and caressing her.

"Please, please," she moaned.

He lifted her and thrust deep, hands gripping her soft, full buttocks. Beth matched him thrust for thrust as they ravaged each other, lost in the heat of pent-up emotions and longing. When they climaxed, it was together, the moon lighting up their blissful faces. Tears ran down her cheeks as she came, whispering, "oh, oh, oh."

Lang's legs shook, but he held her, not wanted to separate, not wanting to leave her warm, sweet depths. "Oh, God, Beth, thank you," he whispered, lips nuzzling her neck. "Are you okay?"

She nodded against him, afraid to speak.

After a long while, he gave her a long, deep kiss and slowly withdrew, setting her wobbly legs down on the soft dirt path. "I'm sorry, darlin'. Wish I was Hercules so I could hold you all night. Where is a boulder or tree when you need one?" In answer, she nuzzled against him and kissed his chest.

After holding each other for a long while, Beth retrieved the flashlight, and they gathered clothes that had been shed in their lovemaking. It took the longest to find her panties, which he had thrown into the tall grass. When he spied them, Lang shouted "Eureka!" and brought them to her, helping her to slip them on. His hands moved up her legs with the silky fabric until they were in place. "Mmm," he said, kissing her bare shoulder. "We'd better start walking, sweetheart. I'm out of condoms, but my body doesn't know it."

She laughed as she felt him harden against her tummy. She reached down and rubbed, just for a moment, before she withdrew her hand.

"Now it's official. Beth Morgan is trying to kill me."

She took his hand. By silent agreement, they began strolling back along the path arm in arm. Lang had the backpack and her sweatshirt slung over his shoulder. When they reached the house, he realized that she had not said a word since their lovemaking began.

"Are you okay, sweetheart?"

"Yes," she said in a soft, tremulous voice. "Thank you for tonight, Lang Dillon." On tiptoes, she kissed him lightly. "I'd better say good night."

"Good night, darlin'."

Beth turned away, took the porch steps two at a time, and disappeared, leaving him standing in the driveway. Deprived of her warmth, Lang felt bereft, a cold creeping over him like nothing he had ever experienced.

CHAPTER 15

"So how was dinner with the most gorgeous new bachelor we've seen in Saguaro in a long time?" Ruthie asked, eyeing her sister. There was something different about Beth this morning. Something Ruthie had never seen in her sister before. If she had not known it to be impossible, she would have sworn Beth had had sex last night. She had that kind of afterglow.

"Don't be silly, Ruthie," Leonora said, waving her coffee mug at her youngest. In a softer voice, she asked to Beth, "Did you have fun, darlin'?"

Frozen, Beth was afraid that if she spoke, it would all come spilling out. Despite the events of the past few days, she had slept like a log and woke wondering if it had all been a dream. The breakup with Bill, meeting Lang Dillon on the road, and mostly last night. She had never done anything so wanton in her life. She shook herself and decided a change of subject was in order.

"Now, Mother, don't faint at what I'm going to say, but where would you suggest I go for a dress for this Saturday? They have nice things at the Outpost and Gabriella's, don't they?"

"Not as nice as Breezy's in Tucson, or Arabella in Prescott. I could go with you? Make a day of it and have lunch?"

"Not today, thanks. Maybe tomorrow. Too much to do at the farm."

"That's cutting it a little close, don't you think?"

"The party's not till next weekend, Mother dear," Ruthie said, sarcasm dripping in her voice.

"Oh, hush, Ruthie. What if she doesn't find something? What if it needs to be altered? Even Maria can't work that fast. She's got a backlog right now with rodeo season coming." Leonora referred to her dressmaker and seamstress, who worked out of a tiny storefront on Saguaro's Main Street.

"Whoa, slow down," Beth said, setting down her fork. Unaccustomed to drinking, her head pounded from the brandy and too many glasses of wine. "Whatever I buy will not need altering, trust me. This is not a grand ball, just a cocktail party. The alternative is to drive home and snatch my little black dress from the condo, but I'd rather not."

"Absolutely not! Why don't we plan to drive to Prescott tomorrow? There's a lovely tea room just down the street from Arabella's. We could have lunch there?"

"Let me try the shops in town this afternoon, see what they have. I might find a perfectly serviceable outfit and save us the trouble."

"My dear, we are not looking for serviceable. We want 'wow.' We want 'dazzling.' We want 'knock their socks off.'"

"No, we most certainly do not," Beth said, sorry she had brought up the subject. "I'm looking for suitable, fade-into-the-background attire. On my best days, I've never dazzled, wowed, or knocked the socks off anyone."

"What about me?" Ruthie said. "What am I, chopped liver? I might like to dazzle."

"You have not gone through the terrible ordeal your sister has, Ruth Ann, but if you'd like to go shopping, I'm happy to take you, too."

Taking one more bite of cold toast, Beth hopped up. "Gotta go. Thanks, Mother. I'll let you know what I find tonight."

"Your father and I are dining out at the club tonight. Carmela will make you girls something nice."

"No, tell her not to bother. Ruthie and I can eat at Gracie's or make sandwiches. Bye."

CHAPTER 16

Lang woke out of sorts, with a headache. Then he remembered the previous evening and what had happened in a moonlit clearing near a meandering stream. He grinned and leaned back, hands cradling his head. He had never experienced anything like that with a woman and wasn't sure how he felt about it, but he knew he wanted it again. Craved it, needed it. Who would have guessed he'd come home to Saguaro and have the most amazing sexual experience of his life?

His father was the only one at the breakfast table when he got down. "Morning, son. How was your date?"

It was on the tip of his tongue to reply that it was not a date, but who was he kidding? The attraction to Beth Morgan had been there since he found her crumpled up like a crushed desert flower on the Gila Road. "Fine. Red Mesa Inn is great. Have you guys been there recently?"

"Not since your mama's birthday, but Chip Redrock runs a first class establishment."

"That's his name, Redrock?"

"Yup. You'd think he was born and bred in the Valley, but he's originally from San Francisco. He and his partner, Jerry Carlisle, came here on vacation. Went on one of the Morgans' pack trips and they've never left. Jerry runs the business end, but Chip's the creative one. They have two award-winning chefs, so that helps the restaurant business."

"Where is Mom, anyway?"

"Went into town, one of her ladies' functions. Your sister left you this sealed envelope and told me not to peek. I expect it's more party preparations, though for the life of me, can't think what else there is to do."

"I'm glad Mom's gone. I wanted to talk to you."

"I'm all ears, but talk fast. I have a distributor coming in an hour, and I've got to be in the office before that."

"Rosie told me what happened, when you broke Mom's jaw."

"It was an accident, son. Ask your ma. She'll say the same."

"I don't give a shit what lies she'll tell me to protect you. I only care about her and her safety."

"Don't take that tone with me, Lang Dillon."

"If you ever hit her again, I'll have you arrested. "

"May I remind you that you're staying under my roof."

"I can easily move to the Red Mesa Inn, if that's preferable."

"Course it's not. Can we drop this? It was an accident. I would never hurt your mother. We've been together forty years, and I love her more each day."

"Then show her and stop drinking. Go to AA, go to a dry-out place, whatever it takes. If you really love her, you'll do it."

Fire blazed in his father's blue eyes, but when he spoke, his voice was calm. "I've gotta go. For your mother's sake, I hope you'll stay on here and not move out in a huff. For my sake, I hope you'll mind your own goddamn business."

Jaybo Dillon pushed open the kitchen door and disappeared before his son could say another word.

"Asshole," Lang muttered as Neecy came through to clear the breakfast dishes.

"Do you want anything besides toast and coffee?" she asked.

"Thanks, Neecy, but I'm good."

He took his coffee and Rose's envelope to the front porch and sat in one of the rockers. As he opened the envelope, his father's truck tore past. Lang was tempted to raise his middle finger, but instead, he pulled out Rose's note and read a long list of party chores she wanted him to do. She ended the note with, *I'll be home late Friday night and we'll go over everything. Thanks, big brother! Love, R.*

"Whoop-de-doo," he said aloud. "Just what I want to do. Plan a party for that bully." *I'm doing it for Mom, not you, you bastard.*

He spent most of the day on the phone and computer, catching up on work. He also called Ben Morgan and asked if there was a good time to meet and talk with him and the stable crew about riding gear. They arranged to have one of the three of them, Harley, Maggie, or Ben, be around to talk Thursday during their lunch break.

Before they rung off, Ben asked, "How was your dinner?"

"Great," Lang said, wary of the other's tone. "Red Mesa Inn is a terrific spot."

"Red Mesa? A bit romantic, isn't it?"

"Valley's only five-star restaurant. Great food, excellent service."

"She's a mess right now, Lang. The last thing I want to see is her hurt all over again."

"I did it to cheer her up. As a friend." *Liar, liar*, he thought.

"My sister's really fragile. I'll do whatever it takes to protect her. You're leaving in a week. All I'm saying is, be careful and don't give her any mixed signals." *What a joke*, Ben thought. It was clear the two of them were sending signals all over the place at dinner the other night. "Stay out of it," Maggie had warned, but how could he?

They rung off on a cordial note, but Lang shook his head, grabbing Rose's list and preparing to head to town. *Just what I need. On top of an abusive, alcoholic father, I now have an angry, testosterone-fueled cowboy breathing down my neck, ready to kill me to defend his sister's honor.* Time to head home to civilization. How many more days until he could make his escape?

Then, there was Beth. It wouldn't be easy to walk away from her. Better to nip this in the bud, he thought. The last thing he wanted was to hurt her. The sex had been incredible, but maybe it was what they both needed: an alcohol-assisted, cathartic roll in the hay? Now they had experienced it. Time to get back to reality, right?

A few hours of mindless party shopping should take my mind of all this, he thought, waving to Neecy as he headed out to the Rover.

CHAPTER 17

The farm was hopping with harvesting, prepping, and planning for Wednesday's slaughter. Beth hated slaughtering days but felt it was her duty to her animals to oversee the process. Raoul handled the field slaughter and bleeding of the steers, and she worked with the crew in the barn as they brought in lambs first, then the pigs.

As truckloads of produce headed to the processing barns, she made a list and time line for the morning's work. She preferred to leave the animals grazing in their familiar surroundings until the very last minute. Then, when Enos arrived, they would head out to walk them in. There were enough of them that the herding was neither stressful nor alarming to the animals. For that, she was grateful.

It was after four when she decided to head into town. *The sooner I get the stupid dress, the better. Otherwise, Mother will insist on dragging me somewhere tomorrow.* She washed up as best she could and unwrapped a new tee shirt from its plastic baggie. One of the farm's newest designs, it was pale blue with white lettering and a silkscreen of produce in a riot of colors emblazoned across it. The only shirt she had in the office was size small, so it hugged every inch of her. She surveyed her reflection in the dust-covered mirror and frowned. "You look like a slut," she said aloud, "but it can't be helped. Only clean thing in this filthy office." *Slut is actually pretty accurate after last night.*

Another transplant to the Valley, Gabriela Huff had started her women's clothing store nine years earlier, specializing in vintage clothes and reproductions of vintage clothes. Now she carried a number of designer labels and some clothes with a local flair—wide bell skirts that twirled, lacy peasant blouses, and billowing tunics that hid a multitude of sins, especially for wealthy vacationers trying to hide flaws and extra weight until they returned home to their personal trainers.

Beth had been in the shop a number of times and had purchased a favorite skirt that she still wore quite often. As she stepped in out of the sunlight, the woman herself emerged from the dressing room alcove. "Well, well, Beth Morgan. You're a sight for sore eyes."

In her late forties, Gabriela had shoulder length auburn hair that cascaded in ringlets over her shoulders. She wore the clothes she sold. Today she sported a mauve lacy top, matching bolero pants, and strappy silver high-heeled sandals. Huge silver hoops hung from her ears, and both forearms jangled with silver bangles. Her violet eyes danced with warmth and curiosity as she came forward to greet Beth.

"Hi, Gabby. Nice to see you."

"Looking for anything special?"

"A couple of cocktail-party-type dresses or outfits. Maybe pants?"

"With your legs, I'd look at the dresses first. What are you, a four?"

"More like a six or eight."

"Nonsense. Let's see what we can find."

They browsed through rack after rack, Gabby chattering the entire time as she pulled out dresses and ensembles, throwing them on the counter. They were the only people in the shop, which helped Beth relax as she began trying things on. The first couple were disastrous in her opinion, although Gabby insisted accessories would make all the difference.

Beth was beginning to despair when she slipped into a silky off-white sheath, overlaid in lace, with strands of silver thread accenting the tatting of delicate flowers. It felt wonderful and fit her perfectly, but since the dressing room had no mirror, she stepped out to stand in the alcove's three-way mirror.

"Oh, my God, it was made for you, hon."

For once, Gabriela's sales talk was right on target. Aside from the dark circles under her eyes and pale, splotchy skin, Beth could not recall a time when she felt prettier and sexier. "I have to say, it feels great."

"And looks like a million bucks! Professor what's-his-name'll probably keel over when he sees you."

"I'm no longer with professor what's-his-name."

"Oh, hon, I'm sorry. What about someone else? Has someone jumped in to take his place?"

"Not really."

"Hmm…I didn't hear 'no.' My advice is—don't pussyfoot around. Get back in the saddle soon as you can."

"Can we just not talk about my love life right now?"

"You got it. Now that we're on a roll, I think we should keep on truckin'."

Beth laughed. "Okay, can you put this one aside and I'll try on a few more. I like that black sheath. I left my little black dress at home."

"Let's try that, then. You start. I'll be right back."

Beth emerged from the dressing room in a black rayon-and-silk sleeveless sheath that felt like a second skin. "This may be a little snug?"

"Nonsense, it's perfect. I have the six, but this is the one."

"Can I at least try the six?"

Gabriela scurried away, returning with the larger size. As always, she was right. The four was much better. They then began accessorizing and wound up with a scarf, two necklaces, bracelets, and three pairs of shoes, two of which were higher heels than Beth liked, but they looked terrific with the dresses. An off-white, open-backed heel for the first dress and a strappy black high-heeled sandal for the sheath. The third pair, which Gabby pronounced to be "boring," were low-heeled black pumps, but they felt terrific. "At least I'll have one pair in reserve, in case I break my ankle wearing one of the other two," Beth called from the dressing room as she threw on her own clothes.

In the course of the marathon shopping errand, she grabbed a few informal tops, two pairs of slacks, and three light sweaters in different shades. With each one, she tried on her usual size. Then Gabby insisted she go a size smaller, "so that they fit ya, for goodness' sake!" The shopkeeper tried to interest her in a shrug, but Beth declared she was not a shrug type of gal.

"Are you ready, hon?"

Beth grimaced, standing at the counter, credit card in hand. When she saw the total, she considered saying "let's forget the whole thing" but then decided, what the hell? So what if the total was more than she made in a week? With the exception of the heels, she felt terrific in everything she had chosen.

Transaction completed, Gabriela passed the bags to her. "You okay, hon? You look pale. It's not spending this much money, is it?"

Beth shook her head, set the bags down and asked if she might sit for a few minutes.

"Course you can, hon. Let me lock the door and put the Closed sign up. Then you can stay as long as you want. I've got at least an hour's worth of work to do before I go home. Can I get you something? Water? Tea?"

"No, thanks," Beth said and bent to put her head between her knees. This was enough to open the floodgates, and she began to sob.

"Oh, my goodness, honey. What's wrong? Can I help?"

"My life, that's what's wrong! Everything I know is gone, vanished. I don't know who I am anymore, Gabby."

"Is it that professor? What'd he do?"

Beth shook her head, unwilling to confide in the gossipy shopkeeper. "He's only part of the problem." *The other is Lang Dillon and me, acting like a wanton harlot last night. I've never done anything like that, ever. It was crazy.*

Gabriela brought her a box of tissues and a steaming cup of vanilla chamomile tea, which she sipped as her sobs slowly subsided. Then the shopkeeper left her alone and went about her work, straightening clothes racks and piles of pants, tee shirts, and sweaters that were in disarray after a day of business. The straightening completed, she went behind the counter to her paperwork.

Finally, Beth stood and grabbed her bags. "Thanks, Gabby. I guess I needed a good cry."

She smiled, giving her a hug before unlocking the door. "Anytime, hon."

CHAPTER 18

Beth threw her bags into the cab of the truck and pulled around the corner to Dixon's for gas. As she replaced the nozzle and waited for her slip, she heard his voice.

"Hey, Beth, just getting off work?" Lang stood on the sidewalk, laden with bags from a variety of stores. The Rover was nowhere in sight.

"Something like that. You look like you've been shopping."

"Rose gave me a list for the big bash."

Keep this light and friendly, he told himself, even though the sight of her in that tight tee shirt made him hard. He moved several of his bags, holding them front of him. As he came closer, he saw her eyes. "Hey, are you okay?"

"Allergies. Been working with hay all day. Does it every time."

Why don't I believe you, Beth Morgan, with those sad eyes and your lovely face covered in red splotches? "How are you?"

"Fine, okay." She dared not look at him. One look into those beautiful eyes and she would go weak in the knees. Less than twenty-four hours ago, he had taken her to heights of ecstasy she'd never known existed. "I'm kind of in a hurry. See you Saturday."

Lang's resolve to nip things in the bud flew out the window, and he covered the distance between them. He grasped her slender arm as she opened the truck door. "Beth, what's wrong? Something's upset you."

Staring straight ahead, she said, "My life is in shambles. Yes, I'm upset. My life as I've known it for ten years is over. I'm just trying to get through each day." She wriggled out of his grasp and slipped into the cab, eyes still averted.

"Beth?"

"I've got to get going, Lang. I'm fine, really." Her voice was softer, but she still refused to meet his eyes.

"See ya, then," he said.

"Yup, see you." She started the truck and pulled out. Only then did she dare look in the rearview mirror. Lang stood watching, his expression perplexed.

Turning, he headed up the street to the Rover. *What the hell was that all about? She couldn't even look at me.* Had last night been that repulsive? Was she going back to Bill and didn't want to tell him?

Lang's resolve to step away completely gone, all he wanted to do was hold her in his arms and kiss away those angry red marks on her lovely cheeks. He would wait until the next day and call her. As he came around the Rover, he spied a flower shop across the street. "And in the meantime," he said aloud, crossing to the shop.

Beth drove home through a haze of tears, not knowing whether they were from the heartache over Bill or the sadness of leaving Lang and his warmth and comforting presence. *He'll be gone next week. Stay away. It's only the few more days. The last thing you need now is another heartbreak.*

When she arrived home, her mother and Ruthie sat on the porch sipping iced tea, a pitcher with several glasses on a tray beside them. "Oh, my goodness," Leonora said, spying the bags. "Did you buy out the whole shop?" Then she spotted her daughter's face. "Sweetheart, what's wrong?"

"Nothing, everything. I seem to be getting really good at crying, and yes, I did almost buy out Gabriela's."

Ruthie watched her sister, concern etched on her freckled face. She was still in her work clothes, jeans covered with dirt, tee shirt stained. She worked with Beth every day but had a hard time reading her. Ben seemed to be the only one who ever got through Beth's thick shell. "Fashion show!" she said, smiling at her sister, hoping a change of subject might help.

"I'll give you a quick peek," Beth said, perking up a little. "Then we can have a fashion show later, okay?"

Ruthie poured her sister an iced tea, and the three spent the next half hour oohing and aahing as Beth pulled one thing, then another from the bags. Finally, the arrival of Ben Senior ended the clothes inspection and they headed in, Beth and Ruthie to showers, their parents to cocktails on the terrace before they left for their dinner at the club.

CHAPTER 19

It was Carmela's night off. She and Raoul had gone into town, but she left a simple supper of enchiladas and salad for Ruthie and Beth. They warmed the enchiladas, tossed the salad, and headed out to eat on the terrace.

"I know we've never been touchy-feely, Bethie, but do you want to talk about it?"

"That's just it. I'm not touchy-feely. That's why Bill and I were so well suited. He isn't, either."

"Maybe that's not a good thing? Maybe you need at least one touchy-feely person in a relationship."

"Is that the way it is with you and Chas?"

"Beth, come on. Chas? Are you serious? Chas makes Bill look like Casanova. Besides, we both know who I'd like to get touchy-feely with."

"What's up with you two, anyway? Why haven't you and Harley gotten together?"

"He's got girlfriends everywhere—all secret, of course."

"How do you know that? I've never seen him with anyone since high school."

"That's because he doesn't date Valley girls."

"Then who?"

"That's the secret part. He goes away to Prescott, Tucson, Santa Fe, California sometimes. Probably's got a woman waiting for him in every town."

"That's ridiculous."

"Maybe, but he's made it very clear that he's not interested in me. Says I'm too young."

"Baloney," Beth said, thinking about the handsome wrangler who, after so many years, was family. "Maybe he's not ready to settle down."

"No maybes about it. And if he and I were to date and he broke my heart, guess who he'd have to answer to? His best friend is our protector, whether we like it or not."

"Tell me about it. I thought he was going to beat Bill into the ground the other day."

"So, what about Bill?"

"I don't know. I've loved him for so long. We were comfortable. I knew who I was with Bill, but now, I don't know. I'm not sure I can ever get beyond seeing him and Skyler in my bed. It's been going on for over a year, you know."

"Men are such jerks."

"Why didn't I see the signs?"

"What signs?"

"I don't know. He must've been acting differently, and I didn't notice."

"There may have been no signs. If someone we love acts a little odd or distant, we don't immediately leap to the conclusion that they're screwing around."

Beth stared at her little sister, smiling slightly. "How did you get so wise?"

"I listen and learn from all my older siblings. I've certainly watched enough breakups, courtships, whatever. Remember when Sam was with Rita? God, that woman called me all the time, tryin' to be buddy-buddy and get inside info on Sam."

Their brother Sam, an architect in Flagstaff, had dated Rita, his dental hygienist, for over a year. Rita was friendly, sweet and pretty, but a bit too aggressive for their quiet brother. He had finally broken things off and then had to change dentists in the aftermath.

"So, what's up with Lang Dillon?" Ruthie asked, studying Beth's face, which registered surprise at the change of subject. As Ruthie watched, her sister blushed crimson. "Uh-oh, something did happen last night. I knew it!"

Beth put down her fork. "Ruthie, can I trust you? If I tell you something, do you promise not to breathe a word of it?"

"Scout's honor," Ruthie said, on the edge of her seat.

Beth swallowed, then began. "Well, we had an incredibly romantic dinner at the Red Mesa, in their private walled garden. Have you ever seen it?" Ruthie shook her head. "We had a lot to drink. When he dropped me off, I didn't want the night to end, so I suggested that we take a walk down to the stream."

"Ooh, that sounds romantic with the full moon and all."

"It was, and that's the problem. When we got there, before I knew what was happening, we were kissing, and a whole lot more. Ruthie, we made love. It was the most amazing sexual experience of my life."

"I knew it! I knew he would be an incredible lover!"

"Incredible doesn't begin to describe it. It was an out-of-body experience. I felt like a different person."

"Do you love him?"

"I don't know! I met the man in the middle of the most traumatic few days of my life. I'm a mess. How can I trust my feelings right now? It's like I threw myself at him to block out the heartache over Bill."

Mouth agape, Ruthie stared at her sister. "You threw yourself at him?"

"Well, not exactly…it was more of a mutual thing, but I was a full participant."

"Oh, I wish I'd been there."

"If you'd been there, it would never have happened."

Ruthie laughed. "That's right. Good thing I wasn't."

"What am I going to do?"

"Are you going to see him again?"

"I just bumped into him in town and practically wet my pants. Got away as quickly as I could. No, I'm not going to see him again. I mean, I'll see him with the party Saturday and all, but not alone again. Too dangerous. He's leaving next week. That's all I need—to fall for someone who can't wait to burn rubber on his way out of town. He hates Saguaro."

"Maybe this'll change his mind?"

"Doubt it."

"I think you should at least see him and talk to him about what happened last night."

Beth shook her head. "I don't think that's a good idea." *If I'm near him, no telling what will happen.*

"Do you think he's in love with you?"

"How would I know? I barely know the man."

"He's pretty cute."

"Yes, he is. Too cute. Bill suited me better. He's solid, nice-looking, but sort of plain, like me."

"Baloney. I mean, I agree about Bill, but not you, sister dear. Wait till you appear in those dresses you bought. Can't wait to see 'em on you. Gabriela has beautiful stuff. Must've cost you a fortune."

"You have no idea."

"That's why you should've gone with Mom. She'd have paid for everything."

"And twice as much. No, thank you. It was worth the price for peace and quiet to decide what I like."

"You know, that's at least the tenth time I've heard your phone ring," Ruthie said. "At least, I think it's your new phone on the kitchen counter, right?"

"Yes, it's Bill, and I don't want to talk to him. I'm gonna turn in. Want to get up early and run before work. Thanks for the touchy-feely, sis."

"No, prob. We should do this more often."

"I hope not."

"I mean, I'm here for you, Beth. Always."

They hugged and Beth said, "Thanks, Ruthie. Remember, mum's the word about Lang Dillon, especially to our big brother."

Beth had just gotten into bed when her phone rang again. Bill, of course. Weary of avoiding him, she answered.

"Beth, hi. Sorry to bother you. I just wondered…I mean, I've been trying to reach you to see if you're free Thursday?"

"Why?"

"Have lunch with me. That's safe, isn't it? I can come up there or we can meet in Tucson. Wherever you say."

"I'm not sure I'm ready to talk to you."

"Please, Beth, I'm going crazy here."

"Fine, I'll meet you at Parson's at one." A favorite sandwich shop right around the corner from their condo, Parson's would be convenient, she thought. Afterward, she could stop by the condo and check on things, grab a few more clothes. That was, if he would not be home. She could not face being in their home together.

She rang off and drifted into an anxious, restless sleep.

CHAPTER 20

Lang called Beth throughout the day, but she never picked up. With each call, he became more and more worried and frustrated. He had abandoned any pretense of nipping things in the bud and now wanted to see and talk to her more than he cared to admit. Was he in love with her? Impossible. Had she had sex with him to blot out the pain of her current situation? He had just picked up his cell to call her again when his mother walked into the study.

"Hey, darlin'. You look like you're working. Are you too busy to drive your old mother into town?"

"When did you want to go?"

"Anytime. It's Tuesday and I need to pick up my weekly order from Freita's, " she said, referring to a gourmet cheese shop in town. "We've ordered so much extra this week for the party that I can use muscle. Neecy would go, but I'd rather have your company."

"Sure, let me finish up a few things. Be ready in twenty minutes?"

"Perfect. I'll be in my office."

Lang punched Beth's number and reached voice mail again. He left a message asking her to call. Twenty minutes later, he and his mother were in the Rover, headed for town.

"So, are you ever gonna tell me how things went with Beth Morgan?"

"Nothing to tell. We're friends, we had a nice dinner, period."

"Lang, darlin' it's me you're talkin' to. No one has a friendly dinner in the private garden at Red Mesa."

"How did you—?"

"This is a small town, darlin'. No secrets here."

Which is exactly why I got out, he thought. "Spies everywhere, then."

"Oh, pish tush. So tell me, what about Beth?"

*****

Beth made the rounds, collected all the lunch orders, called Gracie's and recited everything to Stacy, then grabbed her bag to head into town. It was a tradition on the farm to treat everyone to lunch the day before a slaughter. Beth wasn't sure how it had started, but she felt comforted by the routine that brought everyone together before the long, tough next day. As she planned the day in her head, she almost crashed into Lang and Martha Dillon coming out of Gracie's.

"Beth, hello!" she said. "I was just asking my son about your dinner the other night, but he was very parsimonious in the details. If I didn't know any better, I'd think he had something to hide."

As his mother prattled on, Lang studied Beth, whose face went from pale to green, then bright red.

"Are you quite well, my dear? You look a little flushed." Martha studied Beth, eyes appraising. While her tone was light and chatty, Lang's mother didn't miss much. As she gazed from one to the other, she knew with certainty that something more than friendship was going on between her son and Beth Morgan. *Hmm… she may be a plain Jane, but if she keeps him in Saguaro, I'll be pleased as punch to have her as my daughter-in-law.*

"Beth? Are you okay?" He stepped forward and took hold of her arm. What he wanted to do was draw her close and kiss away the fear and sadness in her beautiful eyes. To feel her softness and warmth against him suddenly seemed like the most important thing in the world.

"Fine. Noonday sun got to me, I guess."

"Why don't we go back in?" Martha said to her son. "Buy this young lady a cool drink and sit with her till she recovers? We're in no hurry, are we, Lang?"

Before he could reply, Beth shook herself and straightened up. "Oh, thank you, that's very kind, but I'm picking up lunch for the crew. They're waiting on me."

"Of course, dear, another time. We're looking forward to seein' you Saturday, but we'd love to have you anytime. Don't be a stranger. Lang, I'm gonna stop in at the post office."

Martha Dillon waved over her shoulder and disappeared, leaving Beth and her son standing, staring at each other.

"Why haven't you returned my calls?" he asked.

Beth stepped back out of Gracie's and closed the door behind her. She scanned the sidewalk for eavesdroppers before answering. "There's nothing to say." *Except that I think I love you, Lang Dillon, more than I've ever loved anyone in my life, and I refuse to let this go on a moment longer. You're leaving and I'm staying and I have to start figuring out how the hell I'm going to live without Bill or you.*

"What about Sunday night?" he asked.

"Sunday night was incredible, but we both know it wasn't real. I'm a basket case. You're leaving next week. What is there to say?"

"So, you were just using me for sex?"

"Don't be ridiculous! I'm not going to talk about this here."

"Then have a drink with me after work."

"Can't. Gotta get to bed early. Tomorrow's a slaughtering day. Besides, I don't think having drinks with you is the best idea."

"Then how 'bout lunch? If not tomorrow, Thursday? We won't have anything stronger than iced tea."

"I'm sorry, I can't. I have to go into Tucson."

"To see him?"

"It doesn't matter. I just have to. Okay, okay, I've gotta go. One drink tomorrow night. Meet at the Bulldog? At six?" She referred to the only saloon-type establishment in town. She chose it because few locals went to the Bulldog. It's patrons were mostly tourists and visitors.

"I can pick you up?"

"No, let's meet there at six, okay? I'll try to get home and shower beforehand, but if not, I may be a bit gamey. We could wait till Thursday at six."

"Tomorrow's fine. I'll take you any way I can get you, gamey or otherwise."

Lang wanted to say more, so much more, but he let her go.

Beth stepped into the cool of Gracie's and breathed a huge sigh of relief. She had seen him and gotten through it without swooning or worse. That was a start.

CHAPTER 21

Beth and Ruthie left the house at five in the morning to get over to the pastures early enough to begin bringing the lambs and pigs in. They liked to move slowly, let the animals meander and graze as they would on any other day. Ben Senior was always chiding his daughters about romanticizing the slaughter and getting too attached to the livestock, but this was the way they liked to do it, and he would never interfere. Their father usually came down at some point during the morning to check in, but he let them and Raoul run the show.

Enos, Raoul, and a couple of local kids were loading the truck when they arrived. After Enos felled the grazing steer most on the first shot, the group moved as one, quickly hoisting the dead animal on a pulley to bleed out. After the four steers were killed and bled, that field would be closed to livestock for at least a month to give the rains and vultures a chance to clean up any trace of the slaughter.

Beth and Ruthie stayed with the lambs and pigs in the holding pens until Enos returned. Their deaths, like the steers', were quick and relatively painless. Once all were slaughtered, the carcasses were loaded into Enos's refrigerated truck and taken to his processing barn in Prescott. He did all the butchering and packaging there. The meat was returned to Morgan's Run by the following day.

The sisters never ate lunch on slaughtering day but paused for a cup of tea after Enos' truck pulled out. Ruthie always cried. Beth seldom did, and today was no exception. Stoic and calm, she walked into the office, heated the tea, took her mug to the back porch and sat, gazing over the fields. When Ruthie joined her, they sat in silence for a while.

Finally Beth said, "Well, that's done. I'm going to spend the afternoon picking strawberries. How about you?"

"Arugula and tender greens. Maybe tomatoes."

It was their habit after a slaughter to spend the rest of the day in one of the fields or gardens instead of among the remaining livestock.

At five, Beth headed in, grabbed her things, and took off for the house, where she showered and changed into clean jeans. She was just about to grab one of her old tee shirts when she remembered the new tops she had purchased. Pulling out a soft sage-green top with low beaded neck, she slipped it on, pleased at the way it hugged her body. She brushed out her long hair, tied it loosely back, applied just a little makeup, and gazed at herself in the mirror, satisfied.

When she came downstairs, her father spied her and whistled. "Don't you look a picture, sweetie? Got a hot date?"

"Hardly. Just meeting a friend in town."

"Anyone I know?"

She hesitated, hating to lie to her father. "Lang Dillon."

Ben Senior smiled. "Well, you'll knock his socks off in that pretty getup, Bethie."

"Thanks, Dad." She kissed the top of his head. "Where's Mother?"

"In the kitchen, gettin' in Carmela's way, I expect. How'd today go?"

"Fine. Enos, Raoul, and the crew did great."

"You, too. Came down midmorning but didn't want to disturb you."

"Well, well, that's more like it," Leonora Morgan said, stepping into the living room.

"Looks like a million bucks, doesn't she, Mama?" Ben Senior patted his wife's behind as she sat on the arm of his chair.

"She certainly does. I may have to stop in at Gabriela's myself. That's a lovely top, darlin', and it certainly suits you. Where are you off to?"

"I'm late, so I'll let Dad tell you." Without waiting for her mother's response, Beth grabbed her bag and scurried out the door.

As she stepped off the porch, she heard her mother saying, "Well, well, well, what's that about?" Beth grimaced, thinking about the third degree that would be waiting upon her return.

CHAPTER 22

Lang arrived early and found a quiet booth at the back of the Bulldog. It had been years since he had stepped into the smoky saloon. Its dark red walls were covered with black-and-white rodeo photos punctuated with racks of antlers and a few stuffed heads. He declined a drink and told the bartender he'd be back when his date arrived. Russ Keeler, bartender and owner, nodded and went back to his work. There were only a handful of customers, all strangers to Lang. On his way to the booth, he grabbed a newspaper from the rack near the bar. It was a local daily and had about two paragraphs of national and international news.

As he flipped through the farm reports and local interest stories, Lang realized he had no idea what was happening in the world. He was reading the schedule for the upcoming county fair when she walked in, hazel eyes scanning the room until she spied him.

He looked up from his reading and smiled, that dazzling smile that made her go weak at the knees. As she strolled the length of the bar, she decided this meeting was a huge mistake. She hadn't eaten anything since breakfast and felt lightheaded and faint. It didn't help that he looked gorgeous as usual, in a soft plaid shirt and jeans, his beautiful blue eyes apprising every inch of her.

Lang's jaw dropped open as he watched her approach. In fact, every man in the place had his eyes glued to her. As she sashayed closer, he noticed every nuance, every breath. Her jeans were worn but fit her snugly, and her tee shirt, or whatever it was, left nothing to the imagination. It hugged her lithe, long frame like a second skin, her soft rounded breasts outlined and peeking out, framed by plunging neckline. *Oh, sweet Jesus*, he thought. *How am I ever gonna walk away from her?*

Lang stood as she reached the table. "Hey, you look amazing and about as far from gamey as they get."

She laughed. "I had time to go home for a shower."

"What'll you have?"

"Beer would be great. And can you ask for some peanuts or something? I haven't eaten all day."

"Do they have food here? Wanta order something?"

"Peanuts would be fine," she said, smiling demurely.

Beth Morgan, I believe you know just how great you look, and you're flirting with me, he thought. "Be back in thirty seconds."

Somehow, Lang Dillon seemed to have turned on a switch inside her. *Steady, girl!* She watched his strong, sinewy back as well as the rest of him as Lang headed for the bar. *This is not you. You don't flirt. You don't even know how to flirt!*

When he returned, he had a pitcher of beer and a basket of peanuts. "They have nachos and wings. Shall I order some?"

"No, these are fine," she said, grabbing a handful of peanuts, shelling and eating them before she dared touch her beer.

Lang watched her, saying nothing, letting her settle in. "Peanuts good?"

"Yes, I needed them." Beth took a swig of beer before meeting his gaze. Why did he have to have those amazing blue eyes? In the dim saloon light, they turned smoky-gray. Deep, mysterious, sexy gray.

"Thanks for seeing me, Beth."

"No problem." She shrugged, trying to keep her tone light and friendly. Who was she kidding?

"So, how'd today go?"

"Smooth, thank goodness. Not my favorite day, but it's part of it."

"And you're off to see Bill tomorrow?"

"Yes."

"For what reason?"

"We need to talk, to settle some things."

"He wants you back, doesn't he?"

"Yes."

"Is that what you want?"

"I don't know. I'm having trouble trusting what I want and don't want right now."

"What about us?"

Beth drank half of her beer, downing it as if she had been crawling across the desert and had finally reached water. "What does 'us' mean to you?"

"I don't know, but I think we should find out, don't you?"

"How? You're leaving next week, and I'm in no shape to explore a new relationship, certainly not a long-distance one."

"The other night was incredible, Beth," he said, voice husky as he reached across the table.

Beth placed both hands in her lap. "The other night was not me. This is not me, either," she said, gesturing to her attire.

"Maybe it's the you that's been waiting to emerge?"

"Don't be ridiculous."

"I'm not. Listen, I felt something with you that I've never felt for another woman. That's something, isn't it?" His eyes pleaded as he reached across the table, palms open.

"I think it was alcohol and lust."

"Bullshit. You don't believe that any more than I do. Listen, I'm going crazy here, Beth."

She downed her beer and poured another.

"You might want to go easy on that if you haven't eaten."

In answer, she took a long, slow drink until half her beer was gone. "I'm fine."

"No, you're not. Let's get out of here and we'll get something to eat."

"I feel like ice cream," she said, downing the rest of her beer.

"Good, let's go." He threw money on the table and stood, holding out his hand to her. She ignored him and jumped up, only to sway back and almost fall into her seat.

Lang grabbed hold of her arm and lifted her, then held her round the waist with his other. "Whoa, sweetheart. Steady now."

"I'm fine." She pushed away from him and staggered toward the door, the sashaying long forgotten.

"Oh, boy," he muttered. "This should be interesting."

CHAPTER 23

They stepped outside, the sun just setting as they walked the two blocks to the Daily Scoop, where Beth ordered a large Moose Tracks cone and Lang, the same. They headed down the street and into the park, where they sat on a bench near the playground. There were a few children playing on the swings, their parents watching from the sidelines, most chatting on their cell phones.

"If ever have kids, I will never do that," he said. "When they're with their kids, why the hell do they need their phones?"

"People find it nearly impossible disconnect," she said quietly. "And, by the way, this is one of the best ice cream cones I've ever had."

"It's tasty," he said. Not a huge fan of ice cream, he would gladly have chucked his in the trash but wanted to keep her company.

"I'm sorry for being such a grouch," she said.

"You're entitled."

"This isn't me at all. I'm usually cool, calm, and collected! All my siblings are the ones who are always shrieking and carrying on."

"Maybe it's time for you to do a little shrieking?"

"It makes me really uncomfortable."

"Beth, you need to give yourself a break."

"Those people are staring at us," she whispered, indicating two women across the playground.

"No, they aren't."

She hopped up and began walking toward the wooded area at the opposite end of the park. A natural formation of boulders sat in the center of a small wooded area that ran to the edge of the park's west side. Without hesitating, she plunged into the thicket and he followed, shaking his head.

When she reached an outcropping, she stopped and leaned against the stone face, still licking the remains of her ice cream cone. "You don't have to stay, you know. We have our own cars. I just felt like we were in a fishbowl out there."

Lang tossed his cone, marveling at how slowly and carefully she nursed hers. "I'll stay. Don't want you to get lost in the woods, never to be seen again."

"Fat chance of that." She gobbled up the last bites of her cone and wiped her mouth with a napkin. She could feel his eyes on her and regretted her decision to escape nosy neighbors by plunging into a secluded spot.

"Beth, talk to me."

Unbidden tears filled her eyes. "There's nothing to say."

"I think there is. I'm sorry. Have I upset you?"

"It's not you. It's everything."

Before she knew it, she was in his arms, sobbing on his shoulder. He turned so his back was to the rock face and pulled her closer. "Hey, hey, it's gonna be okay."

"No, it isn't. It's never going to be okay again."

Whether to stem her tears or because he could no longer control himself, Lang's lips found hers, and he captured her mouth in a deep, lingering kiss. She responded as she wrapped her arms around his neck, pressing against him. Lang silently thanked the crazy voice that had told him that morning to replace his wallet condom. He was already hard and crazy with wanting her, and it was clear she felt the same.

As one hand moved to caress, squeeze, and massage her breasts, the other reached down and unzipped her jeans, which Beth slipped out of, her panties following in quick succession. He pulled her top over her head in one swift motion and slipped off her bra. Her glorious, firm breasts were in his hands, and she moaned, throwing her head back, giving herself to him.

His tongue wove its way down her neck to her breasts, his mouth taking one, then the other, teasing and sucking. Breathless and half crazy with desire,

Beth rubbed against his manhood, first with her body, then her hand. "What if someone comes?" she whispered.

"Who cares?" he asked huskily. "If I'm not inside you in thirty seconds, I'm gonna explode. I've never wanted anyone like I want you, Beth Morgan."

"Take me, then," she said, unzipping his jeans and releasing him. "Condom?"

"Your wish is my command," he said, laughing as he slipped it on, lifted her onto him, and plunged into her depths.

Beth cried out as she rose to meet him. "Oh, Lang," she moaned. "I…I…I love you." Tears sprang to her eyes as she kissed him deeply, begging him to pull her closer, deeper with each thrust.

Lang heard her and almost returned the words, but instead he tried to show her the strength of his feelings through his caresses. His lips were everywhere, on her lips, neck, nibbling at her earlobes, teasing her breasts. As they crashed to climax together, their eyes met and mirrored each other's. Their lips found each other's, and they lost all sense of time and reason.

Afterward, he leaned against the rock face, holding her, closing his eyes, lips trailing soft kisses along her neck. "You okay?" She nodded against his shoulder but said nothing. It had grown dark and the night was cloudy, no moon or stars.

"This is just what I didn't want to happen," she said finally, but made no move to pull away from him. "How could this have happened again?"

"Because, my darling Beth, there's a fierce attraction here, and neither of us is strong enough to resist it."

Suddenly she stiffened. "Can you put me down, please, Lang?"

Slowly he lifted her and pulled out, setting her down gently. "What's wrong? What did I say?"

"I have to get dressed," she said. Fumbling around the ground, she found her clothes and dressed quickly.

"Beth, please don't do this. Talk to me. Don't leave like this. What have I done? What did I say?"

Fully dressed now, she came closer. One hand caressing his jaw, she kissed him long, deep, and slow. "It's what you didn't say that matters, Lang. I can't do this. Please let me go." She turned away and broke into a run.

After Lang collected himself, he followed, but by the time he reached the open field, she was gone. Instead of running after her, he walked slowly, circling the park's perimeter in the growing darkness.

Do I love her? If you can't answer that, buddy, it's time to let her go.

Chapter 24

Beth arrived early to Parson's, hoping to settle into a booth and collect herself before Bill arrived, but he seemed to have had the same thought. She spied him waiting in their favorite booth by the window. She considered asking to change to a different spot, but what was the point? Everything about the place was familiar since they'd eaten there together at least twice a week. At least their favorite booth was somewhat private.

He stood as she approached, leaning forward to give her a quick peck on the cheek. "Hi, Beth. So glad to see you."

He looked tired and drawn. His sandy hair mussed and badly in need of a cut. Deep circles ringed his light brown eyes.

Janice, one of the waitresses they knew well, appeared. "Hey, you guys! I was gettin' worried. Haven't seen you in over a week. You been away?"

Beth forced a smile. "Something like that."

"Know what you want, or do you need a few minutes?

"I'll have a small egg salad wrap," Beth said.

"Reuben for me, thanks, Jan. Two iced teas?" He gazed over at Beth, who nodded as Janice retreated.

"I've missed you." He reached across and tried to take her hand, which she withdrew and set in her lap.

"I'm sure Skyler is only too willing to keep you company."

He pushed his glasses up the bridge of his nose, his habitual response when anxious. "I told you, it's over."

"So, you've had no contact with her except to break it off."

"Give me a break, Beth. We work together. I can't jeopardize her future by firing her from projects she's spent the last few years on."

"No, but you saw no problem in jeopardizing—or should I say *destroying*—my future."

"It just happened, Beth. Please believe me. I am so sorry. My weakness. Nothing to do with you."

"Nothing to do with me?" She paused as Janice delivered their teas. Sensing the tension, she practically threw the glasses on the table and scooted off.

"Nothing to do with me? That's the most ridiculous thing I've ever heard. It had everything to do with me."

"What do you want me to say?"

"Nothing. There's nothing to say. I thought I'd collect a few more things from the condo, if you're not going to be home today?"

"Please don't, Beth. Don't leave me. I'm lost without you."

"Doesn't seem to have bothered you while you were screwing Skyler. Did you think of me while you were rolling around in ecstasy in our bed? Did you even bother to change the sheets?"

"That was the only time we were at the condo, I swear."

"And, we both know your word is rock solid."

"Okay, don't believe me. Think what you want."

The set of his jaw let her know he was furious. "Bill, I don't want to quarrel with you. I don't want to blame you, berate you, anything. I've moved on, and I just want to settle things."

"What's that mean? Have you met someone?"

"That's none of your business, is it?"

"It's that cowboy, isn't it?"

"As I said, none of your business. It's not like we were married or anything."

"Is that what this is about, us not getting married?"

"No, it's about you having a year-long affair with a grad student and me finding you two screwing in our bed."

Beth blanched as Janice set down their sandwiches. Clearly she had heard every word.

"Can I get you anything else, folks?"

"No, thanks," he said. When Janice was out of earshot, he whispered, "I'm sure she heard what you said."

"Good. Then she won't have to worry about why she doesn't see me, but Skyler's seated across from you."

"Stop it, Beth. I said it was over."

"Don't break it off on my account. She can have you. We're over, so if Skyler's your gal, go for it."

"You're the only one for me."

"Bullshit."

"This doesn't even sound like you. What's happened? You've met someone, haven't you?"

"Can we drop this subject, please? My love life is none of your goddamn business. Let's just eat our lunch and go. In a couple of weeks, we can get together and figure out about the condo. It doesn't make sense for me to keep it. I'll probably find something in Saguaro."

"Well, I don't want it, either."

"Fine, then we'll sell. Let's just give it a few weeks and then decide, okay?"

"Fine."

They ate their sandwiches in silence, paid, and stepped out into the glaring sun. Bill walked her to the truck.

"Okay, then. I'll be in touch in a few weeks."

"I can come with you, help you carry stuff."

"No, thanks. I'd rather be alone. It's just a few clothes, anyway."

"Where did you meet him? Is he a cowboy?"

"Goodbye, Bill." Beth slid into the truck and closed the door, refusing to look at him. Only when she had rounded the corner and driven out of sight did she break down. She pulled the truck to the curb and leaned over the steering wheel, sobbing. There was a part of her that wanted nothing more than to say to Bill, "I forgive you. I'm moving home. I want our comfortable life back." But that life was over. Even if she forgave him and moved home, the closeness and comfort would never come back. That life was gone forever.

Finally, she collected herself and drove on to the condo. In ten minutes, she grabbed a few clothes and some toiletries. The space they had lovingly decorated and furnished together felt like a tomb, and the walls seemed to be closing in on her. Finally back on the street, she breathed again.

As she drove home, Beth thought back to the previous evening and her reckless lovemaking with Lang in the village center. Those woods were a favorite necking spot for high school kids. Anyone could have come upon them.

In the heat of passion, she had told him she loved him. Was it true? Or was Lang Dillon a diversion, or worse—a way to get even with Bill?

CHAPTER 25

Thursday afternoon, Lang headed back into town to complete Rose's list of party errands. As he emerged from the bakery, he spied Maggie Morgan and her daughter across the street and waved. They waved and crossed the street as he set the frozen puff pastry in a cooler in the back of the Rover.

"Hi, ladies. Nice to see you."

Emma grinned from ear to ear, skipping in her funny, off-balanced way. "Hi, Lang!"

"Someone's getting very excited about the party Saturday," Maggie said. "How are the preparations coming along?"

"Pretty good." Maggie was one attractive woman. Ben Morgan was lucky. Her daughter was a doll, too. "This is the last of Rose's list. Don't know why the caterer couldn't bring the puff pastry. For that matter, I can't believe we're even having lobster Newberg. I mean, what could be more absurd in the middle of the southwest?"

"Wow, where'd you get the lobster?"

"All shipped from California. We're using langostino and telling my dad it's Maine lobster. He'll never know the difference. It's his favorite dish from when he was stationed in Newport during the navy."

"Then he should have it."

"How's your dad doing?"

"Great. He's semiretired. Still does veterinary work on the side. No more wrangling. He helps out a lot with Emma, which has been a godsend, especially before her dad and I got together."

"Ned Williams was the best wrangler in Arizona when we were growing up. I worshipped him."

She laughed. "I think he'd probably argue with you about the 'best' part, and get a chuckle thinking of himself as someone's idol."

"Then I'd challenge him to name me someone better."

Maggie's dad had spent the better part of his life in the saddle, working for ranches in the area, taking care of large animals on the side. He had gone most of the way through veterinary school but had stopped short of his degree. Over the years, he had kept up with medical advances through any professional development open to laymen. His skills and expertise were highly valued by ranchers and farmers in the Valley, and he was usually the one they called in an emergency.

"Can I buy you ladies a lemonade at Gracie's?"

"Can we, Mommy?" Emma jumped up and down, dancing around her mother.

Maggie laughed. "We'd love it, if you have the time."

"For two beautiful ladies like you, anytime."

When they were settled in a booth, tall ice-rimmed glasses of freshly made lemonade in front of them, Lang asked, "Thursday not a workday for you?"

"No. Since we've been married, I cut back to three days. With Ben back, there's usually plenty of help at the stables. I have cut back mostly to lessons and a few pony camps during the year. Still help out with the mustang program, but my overprotective husband would never allow that now that I'm pregnant."

"What're you doing with mustangs?"

"We train them and domesticate them as much as you can a wild animal. Then they go to the Border Patrol. Those guys are expert riders. They like the challenge and can handle them."

"I've got a pony," Emma said. "I have lessons twice a week."

"Wow, that's amazing. I'd love to see you ride."

"We keep him in our barn. I groom him every day."

"Good for you. I haven't ridden in a while, but I love horses. Grooming's super important."

"Do you still ride?" Maggie asked.

"Not much. I rode when I was in college. A friend roped me into the local polo league a few years ago and I did that for a couple of seasons, but this past year has been too crazy."

"Polo," Maggie said, suddenly looking pensive. "Beth's boyfriend, Bill, is a polo player. They have a league in Elgin during the rainy season when the fields are green."

"I didn't know that." Lang gazed at her. "Is he a nice guy, Sampson?"

"Can I go tell Stacy something, Mommy?" Emma asked, clearly bored with the adult conversation. Midafternoon, there were only two other tables occupied besides theirs, so Maggie nodded.

"Don't bother her, though, okay?"

As Emma ran off, Maggie turned back to Lang. "Yes, he's a very nice man. Until this, he's always been incredible to Beth."

Crestfallen, Lang was not entirely successful in hiding it.

"You have feelings for her, don't you?"

"Obvious, huh?"

"Do you have history? Were you involved before you left Saguaro?"

"No. Of course, I knew who she was. Our parents are best friends, or at least our mothers. Ben Morgan Senior probably thinks my dad is an ass, but that's another story."

The bitterness in his tone surprised Maggie, and she sat quietly, waiting for him to continue. When he did not, she said, "Bill broke her heart. I haven't any idea what she'll do. Go back to him, break it off, who knows? If you're wondering whether I think he's worth it, I cannot say. That's Beth's choice. Bill has always seemed a quiet, self-effacing kind of person to me, and he's been unfailingly kind to Emma and me. He actually took several shifts with her rehab. For that, we— Emma's dad and myself—will be forever grateful to him. As far as what he did to Beth, her brother will never forgive him. But if she decides to go back and try to make things work, we will support her two hundred percent."

"She's lucky to have you in the family."

"We're the lucky ones," she said, hugging Emma, who had just returned with a lollipop from Stacy. 'Thank you so much for the lemonade, but we've got to get going."

Lang said goodbye, and Maggie and Emma departed as he paid. On the drive back home, he wondered if Beth and Bill were still together. Had they made up over lunch? Made appointments with counselors to try to patch things up? *Time to go home*, he told himself. The trip to Saguaro had undone him in ways he had not anticipated. Beth Morgan had rocked his carefully crafted world, and he no longer knew who he was or what he wanted. He thought about her words, whispered in the heat of passion, her soft skin against him, her depths where he had lost himself so completely. Compared to their two liaisons, his sexual life with Cilla seemed like child's play.

CHAPTER 26

With about an hour of sleep the previous night, Beth threw herself into work Friday, determined to let go of thoughts about Bill Sampson or Lang Dillon. Thinking about Bill made her heart ache with loss and emptiness. Thinking about Lang brought fear and confusion at what she would feel next week when he pulled out of town. What had happened to her quiet, predictable world?

At one, she told Ruthie she was closing the office door and taking a nap. "Otherwise, I'll never be able to cope with the onslaught of all the Morgans tonight."

"I hear you, sis. I'm going to be harvesting and weeding the herb gardens all afternoon, so I'll ward people off if I see anyone headed your way."

Beth gave her sister a weary smile. "Thanks, partner."

*****

Kyle Morgan's flight from Boston arrived in Tucson just before noon, and his mother picked him up, immediately peppering him with questions about school and his future. He was midway through Veterinary School in Montana and was thinking ahead to residencies and maybe a transfer for his final years. His mother, of course, was always begging him to come south, but truth be told, he had grown fond of the Boston during his undergraduate years and was thinking of moving back east. He had friends along the coast and he loved the beaches and the craggy beauty of the Vermont and New Hampshire mountains. What the mountain ranges lacked in height and breadth in comparison to the west, they made up for in verdant forests, pristine trails, and the Appalachian Mountain Club huts, where he had worked as crew one summer.

Kyle, Sam, and Ben Morgan looked almost like triplets with their dark hair and brown eyes. Kyle was the shortest of the three. Ben and Sam were both six-four, but Sam, the architect, had the build of the long-distance runner he was, while Kyle and Ben were broad-shouldered and all lean muscle.

"So, what's new around the ranch?" he asked as they headed down the Gila, about ten miles from home.

"Same old, same old. Harley and Ben are organizing a ten-day pack trip for a group of executives from Houston. I believe it's a team-building adventure for them, but we know how those sometimes turn out. The farm's growing every day. Your sisters and Raoul do an incredible job there. Dad and I are making final plans for our trip. I can't believe it's coming up in less than two weeks."

"How's he feeling?"

"Terrific, never better. He's been able to relax with Ben back, which helps. I'm hoping to lure Robbie home soon. Why waste his talents in Sedona when he could be here, leading wilderness adventures for us?"

There's something to be said for escape, Kyle thought, but he smiled at his mother. "How're Ben, Maggie, and Emma liking their new house?"

"Wait till you see it. It's gorgeous. Have you talked to your brother recently?"

"No, why?"

"Well, he has some news, but I won't spoil it. Let him tell you."

Pregnant, Kyle guessed, but he did not press her. "How's my girl, Emma?"

"Thriving. Wait'll you see her. Only has a slight limp, and she's grown so much. It's the only worry I have about the trip. I'll miss my granddaughter terribly, but I don't know what your father's going to do. He'll probably insist we cut the trip short. He's crazy about Emma, spends part of every day with her."

"Can't wait to see her. Is big brother gonna take over all Dad's schmoozing duties at the Lodge?"

"Some, but believe it or not, he's grooming Ruthie for some of it. She's bored in the evenings and likes talking with people. Bought some cute cocktail dresses, too."

"Oh, boy, the tourists don't know what they're in for."

"Hush, now, and don't you go teasing her about it. She's excited and needs a project."

"No progress with her and Harley?"

"Oh, please, that man wouldn't know how to woo a chicken! He's the most exasperating person. Too handsome for his own good."

"How're Beth and Bill? Any wedding bells yet?"

"Oh, dear, I thought your dad or Ben would have called you. Horrible situation." Leonora turned her Escalade into the ranch driveway.

"What's the matter?"

"Well, it turns out that Bill Sampson is a bit of a cad. Beth discovered him with another woman, poor dear. In their bed, no less. She's devastated, of course."

"And he's still alive?"

"That will not help the situation, darlin'. Your father and brother have already threatened to kill him. Harley, too, I believe."

"Good. It can be a joint effort."

"No, it cannot! Oh, look who's on the porch. Sam! I didn't expect him until late this afternoon. Oh, dear, he probably doesn't know about poor Beth, either. And here's your father, too."

Ben Senior drove in and parked the truck beside her. Leonora and Kyle alighted. He grabbed his bags and greeted Sam and their father. Carmela had set a tray of iced tea, glasses, and a plate of cookies out on the front porch table, so Kyle threw his bags in the house, and they all chatted happily, catching up on life and the news about Beth.

Ben Senior grinned from ear to ear, always happiest when his family was together. As he sipped his tea, he wondered if the trip was a good idea. *Maybe we should postpone to be here for Bethie?* He was already missing Emma, and they weren't leaving until next month. He loved listening to the banter of his boys as their mother endeavored to rein them in. When the subject came round to the fate they had planned for Bill, he finally spoke. "I'm hoping Lang Dillon might just take her mind off that Sampson fella. Never good enough for her, anyway."

"Lang Dillon?" Sam stared at his father. "What does he have to do with it?"

"Nothing," his mother said, voice emphatic. "They're just friends."

"Friends or not, they've seen a bit of each other," Ben Senior said. "Good thing, too. She needs distracting."

"Has he moved back to the Valley?"

"No, he leaves next week," Leonora said. "Which is why we are not making more of this."

Unsatisfied, Sam turned to his father, who shrugged. Ben Senior knew better than to contradict his Nora, especially right before a family dinner.

As Sam resolved to ask his older brother and Maggie about the situation, he gazed down the drive, spying his two sisters in Beth's truck.

CHAPTER 27

It was a beautiful night. Carmela and Raoul had set the long table on the terrace, a blaze of color with Leonora's collection of Mexican pottery and her extraordinary linens in shades of blues, yellows, and greens. Robbie arrived shortly before Ben, Maggie, and Emma, and Harley, a de facto family member, had come in last, as usual, bringing a case of excellent California wines with him.

Raoul and Ben manned the bar and grill and kept the margaritas, wine, and beer flowing. Surrounded by her raucous brothers and loving family, Beth felt her frayed nerves soften. No one asked about Bill. She assumed they had all been briefed about her pathetic situation and had been instructed that the subject was off limits. Her parents' doing. She smiled across the table at her father, who had never looked happier.

Noticing his eldest daughter, Ben Senior left off playing with Emma and two of the farm dogs and crossed the terrace to stand beside her, arm circling her shoulders. Beth leaned into his warm embrace. "You're in heaven, aren't you, Dad?"

"You betcha, sweetie. How you holdin' up?"

"Okay. Good to see all the goofballs together. They do get each other going, don't they?"

"Yup. Robbie looks well, don't you think? More like your mother every day, except for his tan."

Fair-haired, with his mother's deep green eyes, Robbie looked strong and fit. The outdoor life in Sedona clearly agreed with him. "Yes, he does. Mom's been at him since the minute he walked in the door to move home and start Morgan's Run Adventure Tours."

He chuckled. "Sounds a bit lowbrow to me."

"Hey, you two," Ben said. He held a pitcher of margaritas. "Beth, you want a refill?"

She shook her head. "Not if I want to make it through dinner."

"Dad?"

"Never touch the stuff, as you well know. Won't say no to another Dos Equis, though."

He held up his empty bottle, and Ben nodded. "Be right back. How're you doin', sis?"

"Fine, just tired. Same as I was ten minutes ago when you asked me. Have you and Maggie told the guys about the baby?"

"Thought I'd announce it at dinner. I suspect Kyle already guessed when he heard Maggie ask for lemonade."

The news of Maggie's pregnancy was greeted with a round of applause and toasting. Emma and Maggie hoisted lemonades, the rest glasses of California pinot noir. The wine complemented the ribs and chicken Raoul had grilled, with three miniburgers for Emma and huge grilled portabella mushrooms for the vegetarians, Ben. Ben looked as if he might burst with pride as he accepted congratulations from his loving family.

Midway through dinner, Sam said to no one in particular, "So, I hear Lang Dillon's around."

Ruthie stole a glance at her sister. "Of course he's around. He and Rose are throwing tomorrow's anniversary bash."

"I'd have thought Martha would have hired a legion of caterers and support staff."

"She has," Leonora said, glaring at her son. "But her children are footing the bill, so they've taken over. I believe Rose has done most of the planning, but since her brother's return, he's pitched right in."

"Thanks to Rose's lists," Maggie said quietly. "Emma and I saw Lang in town the other day and he was very busy, completing his many assignments."

"He's nice," Emma said through a mouthful of french fries. "And funny."

"We had a lemonade at Gracie's," her mother added.

All eyes stared at her, including her husband's. "You didn't mention that," he said.

"Oh, no? Must've slipped my mind, we've been so busy." She smiled at him, hoping he would drop the subject.

"Okay, okay," Beth said, suddenly tired of all the pussyfooting around her life. ""I've seen Lang a few times. He's a nice guy. We're friends. He's been very kind to me. And, yes, Emma, he is very funny. As for Bill and me, I haven't decided what to do there, but I will let you know when I do."

"You're not thinking of going back to him?" Sam asked.

"Maybe, maybe not. I don't know. We've been together for ten years. It's not easy to throw it all away overnight."

"But, Beth," Robbie said before glancing at his father, whose hand was up.

"Can we please change the subject, my chickens?" Leonora said, motioning for Carmela to begin to clear plates for dessert.

The remainder of the meal was spent talking about recent events on the ranch and farm. Harley entertained them with stories of the last two pack trips and the obnoxious city slickers. While Ben Senior did not allow his own children to joke about the paying customers, he had always given Harley more latitude and enjoyed the tales as much as they all did.

Beth was pleasantly tipsy when she finally went to bed. She hoped for a better night's sleep. There were six missed calls from Bill but none from Lang. Apparently, he had taken her seriously and was letting her go. Despite the fact that she had demanded he do so, she was disappointed. Chiding herself, she slipped into bed and closed her eyes.

CHAPTER 28

After watching his sister sleepwalk through a breakfast during which she ate about three bites, Sam decided a distraction was in order. He invited Beth to join him on a couple of errands before he stopped by his brother's and Maggie's. He had promised them he would come over and throw ideas around for the building plans. They were constructing a riding camp for handicapped children. It was Maggie's dream, and Ben Senior had insisted on bankrolling the project and had given it to Maggie and Ben as a wedding present. Sam had already drawn the designs and blueprints, but they wanted to tweak things a bit before the local crew got started.

*****

After much begging and cajoling, Rose convinced her brother to take an early morning ride. They saddled their parents' horses, which were seldom ridden except by the help, who kept them exercised. Rose loved Whimsy, her mother's pinto, and talked soothingly to her as they headed out of the corral. Lang was on Dandy, his father's morgan, bought years ago from Morgan's Run, when the ranch had had an active breeding program. He looked much less comfortable than his sister as they headed for the trail but soon settled into the saddle.

They had decided to take a northwest trail that skirted Morgan's Run and followed a meandering stream, the very same stream where he and Beth had made love for the first time. As they passed very close to the spot where the path from the big house ended, he peered over, curious to view it in daylight.

"What'cha lookin' at?" she asked, looking over at him. "Is there an animal down there? Javelina? Jack rabbit?"

"No, thought I saw something, but it was a tumbleweed."

Rose studied his face. The expression "turned green" came to mind. While he responded in a light, carefree way, his face told a different story. "You okay, Lang? You look like you've seen a ghost."

"Great, never better."

He gave Dandy a kick, and the horse broke into a gallop.

"Whoa, be careful," she called. "It's really steep and rocky up ahead."

When she caught up with him at top of the rise, his face was flushed and he looked himself again. As she studied him, Rose noticed that the clearing in which the horses stood was part of Ben and Maggie's backyard. She pointed up at the house. "What do you think of our old playhouse now? A far cry from when we used to sit on the porch and play house, huh?"

"'Adventure,' sis, not 'house.' Wow, it's incredible. They've doubled the size, at least."

"But doesn't it fit? Fit the land, I mean? They did a beautiful job."

"Who designed it?"

"Ben's brother Sam, with Ben's input, of course. 'Member Sam? He lives up in Flagstaff now. Works for a small firm, mostly residential."

"Yeah, vaguely. Those Morgan men look alike."

As they admired the house and view, they heard the creak of a barn door, and an enormous horse trotted out into an adjacent corral.

"Oh, my God, what's that?" Lang said, watching the enormous creature lumber toward them.

She laughed. "It's Tabasco. Maggie keeps him here now, I guess. Ben Senior gave him to her. He's a draft horse, part Clydesdale. He was one of the wild mustangs, but none of the border patrol wanted to have anything to do with him. He's gentle as a lamb."

"I'll take your word for it," he said, reining Dandy closer as they skirted the corral fence.

At that moment, a voice called hello, and they turned to spy Ben Morgan Junior leading a pony out of the barn, his daughter astride. "Hey, guys. Good morning. Didn't think anyone else got up as early as Emma."

Rose and Lang waved and rode along the fence until they reached father and daughter. "Hey, Emma. What a good rider you are!" Rose called, smiling at the child.

"Hi, Rose. Hi, Lang," Emma called, waving. "My daddy and mommy are teaching me. This is my own pony, Sunny."

"He's a beauty," Lang said, smiling at her.

"Hey, why don't you guys come have breakfast with us?" Ben asked. "Maggie's inside flipping pancakes. She always makes enough for an army."

"Oh, thanks. We couldn't," Rose said.

"Nonsense. Maggie'd love to have you, and I know Emmie and I would, right, Em?"

"Please come!" Emma's eyes danced with delight.

"Well, Rosie, with an invitation like that, how can we refuse?" Lang said. "But we won't stay too long, as we have to get back to Party Central."

"Great, come on in. Tabasco's fine. He won't bother your horses. Or, if you're worried, we can put him in the barn?"

"Might be easier," Lang said, still not entirely comfortable getting any closer to the elephant horse.

Ben grinned. "He's a little intimidating at first. Scared the bejesus outta me the first time I saw him. Course, I was a California boy and had been off the ranch for a while."

As they tied up the horses and headed for the house, following Rose and Emma, Lang asked, "Was is hard moving back? What happened to your business? Do you still run it from here?"

"Thought about it, but then the ranch kind of took over. It was tough 'cause I started it with two of my college roommates, and I really enjoyed working with them. In the end, it was the right decision, though. Too much to do here, and my dad's health isn't great."

"Join the club," Lang said. "Although our dad's failing health is his own goddamn fault. You're lucky. Your father's a great guy and treats your mother like a goddess."

Ben nodded. "They're a love couple, for sure. Only hope I can make my marriage as great as theirs has been. I've certainly found the right woman. Now I just have to be careful not to screw it up."

"Screw what up?" Maggie asked, stepping out onto the back porch to greet them.

"My incredible life," he said, drawing her close for a quick hug and kiss.

Lang watched them, admiring their obvious love for one another. *Will that ever happen for me?* he thought, remembering Beth's soft lips and her gentle touch. "Hey, this house is amazing, you guys. Far cry from the old homestead."

Arm around his wife, Ben grinned from ear to ear. "Well, come on in and we'll give you a tour. Sam and I worked out the bones, but my two beautiful women have decorated it and made it a home."

Home, Lang thought, following the others inside. Would he ever find home?

Chapter 29

After a tour of the house, the group settled down for a sumptuous farm breakfast of pancakes, bacon, and sausages. Ben proudly told them that every ingredient except the maple syrup, had come from the Valley. "Not the healthiest breakfast in the world," Maggie declared, "but we figure once a week won't kill us."

Lang regaled them with stories of working on friends' Vermont farms, helping tap the maple trees and harvest the syrup. He promised that the next time he visited his friends, he would send them a case of maple syrup. "And maybe a few packages of maple sugar candy," he added, winking at Emma.

Plates empty, they were chatting when the front door opened and they heard Sam call, "Hello, anyone here?"

"It's the genius himself," Ben said to Lang. "You can ask him all those questions you were asking me that I couldn't answer. Sam brought his own foreman and construction crew from Flagstaff. It ruffled a few feathers in town, but we used local guys to build the barn and outbuildings, so that smoothed things over a little. Hey, brother, we're back here!"

Sam Morgan stepped into the kitchen, a thinner, leaner version of his older brother. Lang watched Rose blushed crimson when she spied Sam. Lang was so busy wondering about Rose's reaction to this handsome Morgan brother that he failed to see who followed Sam until Beth bent to hug Emma. She looked especially lovely in a pale blue, faded work shirt and jeans that hugged her curves. Her hair was tied back in a loose ponytail.

Maggie looked around and marveled at the change in the room. "We just finished, but I can make more pancakes. Have you guys eaten?"

"Yup," Sam said, stepping round the table to give Rose a peck on the cheek. He then extended his hand to Lang, whom he noticed had not taken his eyes off Beth. "Hey, Lang, it's been a while."

Shaking himself, Lang turned and shook Sam's hand. "Good to see you. This house is amazing. Your work is amazing."

"It was a joint effort," Sam said, smiling as he glanced at his sister. Beth's face had drained of color, and her lips quivered. "On second thought, maybe some coffee and toast might be good. What'dya think, sis?"

Beth took a step back, leaning against the counter, trying to compose herself. "No, thanks, I'm fine." She'd been preparing herself to see Lang at the party, but this unexpected encounter left her reeling. How could anyone look this gorgeous at eight a.m.? Lang wore a gray Rambler Sports tee shirt and faded jeans, possibly the same faded jeans she had practically ripped off him two nights ago.

Yeah, right, Ben thought, watching her. "Sit down, sis. Have something." He gave her his chair and Beth sat, hard. Oblivious to her aunt's distress, Emma began regaling her with stories about her riding success and how she was training Sunny. Beth breathed deeply and gave her full attention to her niece.

Lang wasn't sure who looked worse, Beth or his sister, but he decided that now was the time to exit. Beth's distress was lost on no one, least of all her lover, who stood and said, "Rosie and I need to get cracking. Martha will send out the posse if we aren't back soon. We've got a million things on the list before tonight, don't we, sis?"

"I'll walk you out," Ben said, winking at Maggie and Emma as he headed for the back door.

Flustered, Rose stood and looked around at her companions, unable to meet Sam's eyes. "Thanks so much for breakfast. It was terrific."

"Ditto," Lang said, coming around the table to stand beside Beth's chair. "I guess we'll see you tonight, huh?" He addressed them all, but he only had eyes for Beth. "Have a great day."

His hand on the back of her chair grazed her shoulder as Lang stepped back. Beth flushed crimson and sputtered, "Of course. Looking forward to it."

"Well, then, that's settled. Be right back," Ben said, hurrying their guests out the back door. Emma followed, skipping along in front of the three adults to see her pony.

As the door closed, Maggie looked from Sam to Beth. "You guys okay?"

"Fine, now," Beth said, letting out a huge sigh.

"Fine, never better," he said, grinning. "Why do you ask?"

"Because there was something cooking in this kitchen between four people, and that didn't include Ben, Em, and me. What's going on with you and Rose?"

"Nothing." Sam shrugged. "I mean, Rose is great, but she's a friend."

Friends don't blush to the tips of their ears when they greet one another, Maggie thought, turning to Beth. "You okay, sister-in-law?"

"Gettin' there."

"What's going on, Bethie? Are there suddenly two guys your brothers need to whip?"

"No, and nothing's going on. Lang and I are friends."

"Yeah, right," Sam said, but he dropped the subject, rolling his eyes at Maggie, who was wiping the table.

Sam spread out the blueprints, and the three leaned into them.

*****

Ben walked the Dillons out and helped them onto their mounts. "You gonna take a ride before headin' back?"

"Maybe a short one," Rose said, heading for the barn to say goodbye to Emma. "Thanks again."

"She's a mess right now," Ben said, gazing up at Lang.

"I know."

"We don't want her hurt any more than she already is."

"Neither do I, believe me."

"What's going on, then? She looked like a scared jackrabbit facing a coyote."

"I don't know, but if I had to guess, it's lack of sleep."

"I was with her last night, and she wasn't acting like that. Not till she spied you."

"We're friends. There is an attraction, but I know what's she's going through, and I'm tryin' to keep my distance."

"Good. Well, let's hope it stays that way. Have a good ride."

Great, Lang thought as he and Rose set off. *The Morgan boys are circling the wagons, ready to string me up.* He had promised and he would stay away, but he missed Beth Morgan—in fact, ached for her with a hunger he had never experienced before.

CHAPTER 30

Beth dressed carefully in the silky off-white sheath overlaid in lace, its strands of silver thread and delicate, silvery flowers accented by shimmering silver earrings and a Navaho silver bracelet. Round her neck, she wore a small silver locket that held strands of her baby hair. It had been her first birthday present from her parents and was Beth's favorite piece of jewelry.

She applied a dab of mascara and lipstick, then slipped on the off-white open-backed heels Gabriela had begged her to buy. As she wobbled down the stairs, she thought, *After my entrance, if I don't fall flat on my face, these heels are history.*

Her parents and three of her brothers, dressed and ready, were sitting round the living room.

"Wowee, sweetheart," her father exclaimed. "Don't you put the sun to shame."

Her brothers whistled, and Leonora cried, "Now that's more like it! I'm gonna have to give Gabriela's another try if she has dresses like that. You look gorgeous, my darling."

Ruthie appeared at that moment. Her curve-hugging dress was a soft blue that matched her eyes, and she wore high heels. Her red hair was swept up in a chignon, and her face was transformed by subtly applied makeup and lipstick. "Hey, what am I, chopped liver?"

More whistles and compliments from their parents followed her entrance, and then the group set off, all piled into Leonora's Escalade and Sam's Volvo Cross Country SUV.

*****

The Dillons' backyard was covered with tents, each decorated with twinkling lights, and extravagant floral arrangements. The main tent housed tables and a huge dance floor. Two smaller tents held the buffet tables and bar. There was a second, smaller bar at one end of the big tent, stocked with wine and beer.

Their parents were still dressing as Rose and Lang mingled among the caterers, checking on last minute details and greeting the first guests. Rose was in soft pink, a sleeveless sheath that flattered her thin, lovely figure. A single strand of pearls at her neck and matching earrings were her only adornments. She wore sensible but expensive off white flats.

Lang gave her a wolf whistle when he spied her, then frowned when she donned a striped Saguaro Valley Winery apron. "What're thinking, sis?"

"I'm thinking 'Don't get this dress dirty before people get here.' I'll take it off, don't worry. You're looking pretty cute, brother dear. Did you get that suit in Boston?"

Lang wore a pale gray suit with subtle pinstripe, a blue dress shirt and, against his wishes, a Saguaro Valley Winery tie, which his mother had begged him to add. He had to admit, the colors did match the suit, even if he hated to be a walking advertisement.

"New York, last fall. Brooks Brothers end-of-summer sale."

"Ladies'll be swooning."

Lang followed his sister, making ineffectual attempts to assist as guests began trickling in. An hour later, over two hundred people filled both tents, sipping champagne and all manner of drinks. Except for the champagne, all the wines were from the hosts' winery.

The Morgans arrived in two waves, the group from the main house followed by Maggie, Ben, Emma, and Ned Williams, Maggie's dad. Lang greeted Ned, genuinely glad to see him. They began a spirited conversation as the others dispersed.

True to his word, Lang greeted all the Morgans, including Beth, then stepped back and kept his distance. *It's much harder tonight with her in that dress.* Her lithe beauty took his breath away. Swamped with well-wishers, he was swallowed up in the crowd and lost sight of her. Aside from staying away from Beth Morgan, Lang had appointed himself watchdog over his father. He intended to keep track of how much Jaybo had to drink and monitor his behavior. So far, his parents had been so busy, they barely had time to grab a drink, and each one that was passed to them soon landed on a table or tray and disappeared after sip or two.

For her part, Beth mingled, staying close to her brothers and in the background as much as possible. Ruthie was on the dance floor immediately, dancing alone, with friends, or with anyone she could grab. She had attempted to drag her sister out, but Beth refused and stayed firmly planted at the edge of the crowd. Lang had given her a warm hello, then disappeared. Incredibly handsome in a suit that hung perfectly on his lean, sculpted frame, one look into those blue eyes and she nearly swooned. Mercifully, he had vanished quickly, allowing her to regain her composure. She now found herself scanning the crowd, hoping to catch a glimpse of him.

"Having fun, baby doll?" Her father hugged her, and she leaned against him.

"Not especially."

"Want to come sit with the oldsters? Your mother has commandeered a table for all her Cowbelles, and I'm sure we can squeeze you in."

"Thanks, Dad, but I put my stuff with Maggie and Ben."

"We're right near the bar if you change your mind, sweetie." He bent and kissed her cheek.

"Thanks, Dad."

After extracting himself from a very attractive redhead's embrace, Robbie sidled up. "Wanta dance, sis?"

"Who's your friend?" she laughed, allowing him to lead her to the dance floor.

"Bella Campbell. She was in my class. She's single and on the prowl."

"Cute."

"Cute like a cougar."

They danced several fast dances, mostly country-western songs. Then the band played a slow waltz, and Kyle cut in as Robbie headed for the bar. "How you doing, Bethie?"

"Fine, now that I've ditched the heels."

As they cruised around the floor, they noticed Sam dancing with Rose. "Something's cooking there," he said. "That's at least their tenth dance."

Beth was glad. Rose Dillon was a kind, smart, wonderful person. Now if Sam would only recognize and appreciate that. He tended to date what her brothers dubbed "flaky airheads." Beth had liked many of Sam's girlfriends, but she was now rooting for Rose.

So intent were they in watching Rose and Sam, Beth didn't notice Lang and a buxom blonde until they almost bumped into each other. The blonde was pressed against him, shamelessly sliding to and fro, rubbing him up and down. Her red chiffon dress looked as if it had been painted on.

Kyle nodded at Lang, then waltzed Beth away. "Looks like Dillon's found a friend."

"Who is she?"

"Dunno. Looks vaguely familiar, at least from the backside."

Beth punched him playfully and they laughed, but inside her stomach was tied in knots and she felt sick. "Okay if we head back to the table for a bit?" she asked. "I think I need to eat something."

"Sure thing. I'm with ya."

Kyle led her back to their table. He had seen her expression, the pain and hurt, as Lang and his bimbo waltzed by. Something had happened there, and he sure wanted to know what.

CHAPTER 31

As Beth moved down the buffet line, Kyle veered off to talk with high school friends. She had just served herself some salad and a tiny portion of Mr. Dillon's lobster Newberg when she saw Lang, plate in hand, heading toward her. Afraid she might be tempted to throw her plate of food in his face, she set it at the back of the table. As she turned, he spied her and smiled.

"Where's your lady friend?"

"Who?"

"The blonde you've been… Oh, never mind. I really don't want to know."

His liquid blue eyes gazed at her, full of concern. "Beth, what's wrong?"

"Everything. Nothing. I don't know. All I know is that you've been avoiding me like the plague. And now you're flirting shamelessly, right in my face."

"What are you talking about? You asked me to let you go and leave you alone. It was not my choice, but I'm trying to respect your wishes. You look incredibly beautiful tonight, by the way, so staying away has been torture."

"What was it, Lang? Grab the clueless farm girl for a roll in the hay, a little diversion during your quick stop in the Valley? Wine her, dine her, and she'll do anything."

"That's bullshit and you know it. First, you're hardly a clueless farm girl and, as I recall, you were a full participant in our lovemaking. I never heard 'stop, Lang.' Second, I saw a friend who was hurting, and I wanted to help."

"Well, you certainly went way beyond friendly!" Tears sprang to her eyes, and Beth turned away.

He took her hand. "Beth, I'm sorry. This is probably not the best place for this. Do you want to take a walk?"

"That's the last thing I want to do with you, Lang Dillon. Let go of my arm."

He released her just as Kyle approached. 'Everything alright here, guys?"

"Fine," she said. "And don't you start, either." With that, Beth reached over, grabbed her plate, and headed for the table where most of her siblings had gathered.

Beth sat next to Maggie and glanced around the table. Except for Ruthie, who was dancing up a storm with some friends, all of her brothers were staring at her. The only one who seemed unaware of the recent scene with Lang was Emma, who was chattering happily to Robbie. Setting down her plate, Beth looked at each pair of eyes. "Okay, everyone. All is well, and I do not want to hear one word about what just happened. Are we clear?" She received a chorus of nods and a few mumbled yeses in reply. "Good!" She plunged her fork into her salad and forced herself to eat a few bites.

Shaken, Lang went to check in with Rose, who was conferring with the caterers about the desserts. There was a huge cake in the shape of a map of the property. Made by the Bakery on Main, it depicted the winery, fields, houses and outbuildings. "Forty Years of Partnership" was emblazoned across the middle. Lang thought it was the tackiest thing he had ever seen and Rose agreed, but their father had insisted on it as a surprise for his wife. Both brother and sister suspected their mother would feel as they did about it but would put on a brave face.

"What's the matter with you?" Rose asked, noticing her brother's expression. "Everything okay?"

"No, but there it is. This is why I avoid the Valley like the plague."

"What happened?"

"Nothing. Beth's pissed that I'm avoiding her, which is what she asked me to do—leave her alone."

Rose patted his arm. "Poor baby. You haven't learned much about women in thirty-four years, have you?"

"Apparently not. Let's drop it for now. You can give me the woman's perspective later. Is it time to unveil the monstrosity?"

"Not yet. People are still eating dinner. The caterer thinks in about a half hour."

"Do I really have to give a toast? Don't want to say one thing about the bastard."

"Lang, please. This is for Mom."

"Sorry, sis. I'm an asshole."

"No, you're not. Now, tell me, who was that blonde you were waltzing around?"

"Don't you start. Didn't you recognize her? Jackie Peltzer. She was a year ahead of me in high school. A brunette then. Her father's one of Dad's biggest customers. Wine distributor, lives in Phoenix. Jackie works for him, apparently. She's invited me for a visit."

"Lucky you. You going?"

"Yeah, right. I have enough women troubles. I certainly don't need that cougar breathing down my neck."

Rose laughed. "I suspect she'd be doing a lot more than that!"

"I'll get you for that, sister dear. You know, I could start about you and Sam Morgan, but I'm too much of a gentleman."

Rose blanched. "Gotta go up to the house for a sec. Keep a lid on here and practice your toast."

"Can't wait."

As Rose disappeared, two of his father's golf buddies found Lang. Taft Granger patted him on the back. "How's life in the fast lane back east, son?"

Lang chuckled, genuinely glad to see the two men. "Not as fast as here."

"Oh, do tell," Ollie Packer said, signaling to the waiter for another Scotch.

CHAPTER 32

After several largely futile attempts to force herself to eat, Beth excused herself and told Maggie she was headed for the ladies' room. The Dillons had brought in a row of luxurious Porta Johns that resembled fancy marble bathrooms, complete with dressing tables and baskets of toiletries. Midway across the tent, Beth was just maneuvering around a dancing couple when she saw Bill framed in the main entrance to the tent. Aghast, she paused, uncertain of whether she should turn and run or move forward. She chose the latter course and hastened to intercept him.

At this same moment, Ben Senior also spied Sampson, as did Beth's siblings, even Ruthie, who paused in her dancing to stare.

"How dare he?" Ben Senior said, as he started to rise.

Leonora grabbed his arm. "No, Papa. Let her handle it." She caught the eye of Ruthie, who nodded, circling around the edge of the tent toward the couple.

Ben and his brothers rose as one, but before they could move an inch, Maggie raised her hand. "No, leave them be. This is one time when the Morgan boys' intervention is not required. Your sister's strong. She can handle it."

"That bastard has a lot of nerve showing his face after I told him to stay away from her," Ben said as Maggie put her hand on his forearm.

"Ben Morgan, if you move one step, I'm leaving and taking Emma with me."

Her husband sat, as did his brothers, but if looks could kill, Bill Sampson would be dead as a doornail.

"Jerk," Robbie said, shaking his head.

"If she starts crying, Mags, all bets are off," Kyle said, slapping his napkin on the table.

"Okay, we all agreed," Sam said. "If she cries or he makes any false moves, we whup him good."

"Spoken like a true cowboy," Maggie said. "Where's Harley, anyway? We'd better make sure he's corralled."

"Ruthie's got him," Robbie said. "They're together over there, ready to pounce if needed."

Beth reached Bill just as he spotted her. She cringed, wondering if her brothers were watching. "Bill, what in the world are you doing here?"

"I was invited, remember?" Except for the dark circles still under his eyes, he looked especially handsome, hair trimmed, with a new tie and green dress shirt. He wore a beige linen suit he had recently purchased for their ten-year anniversary this coming fall. They had planned a trip to the Grand Canyon and a fancy dinner at their favorite restaurant in Flagstaff on their way.

"Do you know what my brothers will do if they see you?"

"I'm not intimidated by the Morgan boys."

"Well, you should be."

"I see them at the table. It appears Maggie has called down the posse. You look very beautiful, my darling."

"You don't get to call me that anymore," she said, thinking how comforting it would be to fall into his arms and erase the past week from her memory.

"One dance and I'll go," he said, extending his hand as strains of Whitney Houston's "I Will Always Love You" reached them.

"One dance," she said softly, and took his hand. *It would have to be this song!*

Rose found her brother just extracting himself from conversation with Ollie and Taft. Lang pointed to Beth and Bill and said, "Is that who I think it is dancing with Beth?"

"You met him, I thought?"

"Only for a second."

"He's a nice-looking man," she said, smiling at her brother. *A little jealousy won't hurt him*, she decided.

Bill drew her close and Beth stiffened, pulling back.

"Sorry," he whispered. "Force of habit."

They moved slowly, in tune like the long time couple they were, familiar with each other's rhythm. Dancing was something they both enjoyed, and many Friday nights they went to one venue or another, trying everything from contra dancing to swing. One of their favorite spots was a lounge that featured ballroom dancing where patrons moved and swayed to the music of the 1930s and 1940s.

Beth closed her eyes and let herself be led, giving body and soul over to the music. *Let go of the hurt and quarrels for three minutes. Let yourself be happy and at peace.*

As Lang watched them, his chest tightened to the point that he wondered if he were having a heart attack. Beth looked blissful, the haunted, scared face of the past week fallen away. She was in the arms of the man she loved. She loved Bill Sampson, not him. Disgusted, he turned and left the tent. He grabbed a bottle of champagne from the bar and walked out into the night. If he had remained, he would have seen the change in Beth as the last strains of the song reached her. Tears filled her eyes as she opened them, stop swaying, and gazed up at Bill.

"I loved you, Bill, with all my heart. I never doubted for an instant that we would grow old together."

"We still can, Beth. Please forgive me. That's what I want. To grow old with you. To love and cherish you. If you want to get married, let's do it. Now, tonight, tomorrow, next week, whenever you say. I was a stupid fool for not asking you sooner."

Beth stared at him, almost feeling sorry for him. She reached up, and her hand caressed his face as she ran her finger along his square, handsome jaw. "It's over Bill. I'm not coming back. We can sell the condo or you can buy me out. Let's find a time to talk in a few weeks, when you decide."

"Oh, God, no, Beth, please don't say that. I'll do anything."

"There's nothing to do. It's gone. My love for you is gone, and it's never coming back. I saw Skyler that morning, but I also saw you and your face. There was something there that I've never seen. An aliveness, a vitality. Go back to her. Make it work. We're over. Goodbye."

Not waiting for his reply, she turned her back and walked away, straight to the table with her family. Bill watched her go, then turned and left.

No one at the table said a word. Maggie took her hand, and Ben's arm circled her shoulders. As Ruthie and Harley left their post and crossed the room to join them, Emma crawled down from her seat and came to sit on her aunt's lap, her tiny arms wrapped around her waist. Beth rested her head on Emma's curls and wept.

Ben Senior started to get up, but Leonora stopped him again. "Let her be, Ben. She's okay, and her brothers and sister are looking after her. There'll be time for her Mama and Papa when we get home." Ben Senior kissed his wife and nodded, sitting back down.

CHAPTER 33

As Beth and Bill danced, Lang had drifted away from his sister's side. Now Rose scanned the room, but she couldn't find him. She headed toward the one of the smaller tents, and the bartender told her Lang had grabbed a bottle and headed down the lawn. She found him sitting on a teak bench under a grape arbor, one of the few on the property that grew jam and jelly grapes. The champagne had not been corked.

"Hey, son of the happy couple. Time for the cake and your toast."

"I can't, Rosie. You'll have to do it."

"Oh, no you don't. You're not pulling that on me."

"Screw it."

Rose sat beside him. "Lang?"

He turned and looked into her lovely hazel eyes.

"She sent him packing," she said softly.

"What are you talking about?"

"You know very well what I'm talking about. The woman you love had one dance with her old boyfriend. It ended and she told him to get out of her life forever."

"How the hell do you know that?"

"Body language, for one, and I was also standing about six feet away when the dance ended. I heard every word."

"I'm not in love with her."

"Lang Dillon, this is me you're talking to. You forget, I can read you like a book."

"Not anymore. I've changed."

"Baloney. Now, are you gonna come back and give that toast or am I gonna tell all our guests that you refused to toast our dear mother and father on their special night?"

"Fine," he said, setting the unopened bottle on the bench. "But I'm leaving this here and coming back right after the toast to guzzle the whole thing."

When the toasting began, Rose spoke first and introduced her brother, a stranger to many who did not remember him as a youth or teenager. Then Lang stood, kissed his sister's cheek, and moved to the mike.

"Rosie and I have been blessed with a beautiful home and loving parents. Our mother, Martha, is the most caring, generous person I know. For our entire lives, she has been an extraordinary role model, friend, and beloved caregiver. She is also a devoted wife to our dad, Jaybo, who built this ranch from scratch, with his loving partner at his side. Love is an alchemy that transforms the ordinary to the extraordinary, the mundane to profound, the average to the exceptional. I hope they continue to have it and that their next forty years find them cherishing the time they have together and cherishing each other. To Martha and Jaybo!" He raised his glass and smiled at his mother, then Rose, never once meeting his father's eyes.

A few more people spoke. Then Martha and Jaybo cut the cake, and the caterers passed trays of desserts and coffee.

Lang found Rose as she supervised the cake cutting. "Can you handle things for a while? I've got a bottle of champagne waiting for me."

Rose turned to her brother, fury in her eyes. "I never thought the day would come when I'd say my brother was a coward. Go ahead, get drunk. Drown your sorrows in a bottle just like dad. What a hypocrite you are, Lang Dillon."

Rose grabbed a piece of cake and stalked off, leaving him alone. Lang watched the one person he could always count on fade into the crowd. To his recollection, he had never seen his sister lose her temper, much less at him. He didn't notice Harley Langdon standing beside him until the other spoke. "She's a spitfire, isn't she?"

"Not usually."

"She's right, you know?"

Lang gazed at the man he barely knew, wondering at their strange conversation. "About what?"

"Whatever you were talking about. Buddy, if you haven't learned it yet, time to wise up. If you want to survive in this world, you've got to wrap your head around one very important fact—women are always right."

"That might be true if the women stuck with same story, but it's been my experience that they change the rules every five minutes."

Harley chuckled. "Yeah, there's that, too."

"You have someone in your life?"

"Not really."

"Looked like you were having fun with Ruthie Morgan."

"Like a little sister to me."

"Yeah, right. I may not know much about women, but I know chemistry and attraction when I see them. Not all coming from her, either. You're busted, buddy."

Harley grinned and stared off into the crowd. "Maybe. So, what's going on with you and Beth?"

"Did the Morgan boys send you?"

"No, but I'm of the same mind as they are. She's like another sister."

"For the last time, there's nothing going on. We're friends, but we got a little too friendly. She asked me to back off, and I have."

"And now she's mad that you did."

"Exactly."

"Well, you want my advice?"

"Not especially, but what the hell."

"Not sure how long this shindig's gonna last, but my advice would be to ask her to dance before it's too late."

"How is that going to work?"

"Look, she danced with her ex and she hates him. I think you'll be safe."

"You're kidding, right? This is some elaborate setup to earn me a slap in the face, then a beating from her brothers, isn't it?"

"Ask her. I'll handle them. And if you get slapped, you can slap me."

Lang laughed, looking over at the other man, uncertain whether he was serious or just setting him up. "Okay, but don't say I didn't warn you."

Harley patted him on the back. "Good luck, man. You're gonna need it."

Yes, I am, Lang thought as he made his way along the edge of the crowd of dancers until he neared the table where Beth sat. Maggie and Emma were dancing with Ben, and Sam was once again with Rose. Kyle, Robbie, and Beth sat, eyes toward the dance floor, enjoying watching Emma skipping with delight.

"Uh-oh," Kyle said, nudging his brother. "Look who's headed our way."

At that instant, Ben spied Lang and made a move toward the table until Maggie grabbed him. Beth was so intent on watching Emma that she failed to notice Lang's approach until he stood next to her chair.

As the music changed and the band began playing Armstrong's "What a Wonderful World," he held out his hand. "Dance with me?"

She took his hand and stood, allowing him to lead her to the dance floor. As he slipped his arm around her and pulled her close, every Morgan in the room as well as Harley and Rose watched their every move.

"Now I know what a fishbowl fish feels like," he said, smiling down at her.

Beth looked like a scared rabbit, so he added, "Relax, it's just one dance. You're perfectly safe. If I make one false move, there are at least five men, maybe six, including your dad, who will beat me to a pulp."

Gratified, he felt her relax against him as she rested her head on his shoulder. "That's better," he whispered as he drank in the scent of her, desert roses and sweet clover. He drew her against him and swayed to the music of Louis Armstrong, wishing that the beautiful ballad would never end.

"I wouldn't let them beat you to a pulp," she said, nuzzling his neck, happy and peaceful. *He may leave you next week, Beth Morgan, but he's here now, holding you. Let that be enough, at least until the song ends.*

When the song was over, the band leader announced, "That's it, folks. Have a great evening. It's been a pleasure."

As the crowd applauded, Beth and Lang held each other close for an instant before she pulled back, feeling a wrench at leaving his warmth behind.

"Thanks," she said. "I think my ride is getting ready to leave."

"Can I drive you?"

"I'd better go with my family. Besides, I'm sure Rose needs you here."

"Probably." He took her hand. "Listen, Beth, this is ridiculous. Can we get together, maybe tomorrow, and talk about this?"

"I don't know, maybe. Let me sleep on it."

The scared rabbit look was back. She was terrified of being hurt. Could he guarantee that she wouldn't be? His feelings were inside out and upside down, and the last thing he wanted was to cause his beautiful desert rose more pain. "I've got an idea. Why don't you decide? If you'd like to do something, give me a call. Maybe a quick, casual lunch or dinner, a ride? I'm pretty much a tenderfoot, but it sure was pretty out there this morning, and Rose and I didn't get far."

"I don't ride much."

"So, does that sound good? You'll let me know if you'd like to do something?"

"Okay. Good night."

She let go of his hand, and his chest constricted as if someone had torn out his heart. Had he ever felt this way with Cilla? Not that he could remember.

CHAPTER 34

Lang and Rose stood with their mother, saying goodnight as guests strolled out into the night. Their father was at the far end of the tent, talking with a group of ranchers. Rose stood between her brother and Martha, aware of the tension mounting on either side of her. She had witnessed Lang's dance with Beth Morgan, and she had seen her father stagger out of the bar tent over an hour earlier.

"You okay?" she whispered to Lang.

"I'll be better when he's in bed and Mom's safe."

"Hush!"

"He's drunk, isn't he?"

"I don't know."

"Bullshit, Rosie. I'm not the only one who's been watching him reel around all night."

She elbowed him as her mother stared at first one, then the other. "What are you two whispering about?"

"Nothing, Mom" she said, patting her arm. "Did you have fun tonight?"

"It was lovely, darlin'. The loveliest party I've ever attended."

"Good," Rose said, nodding to the guests filing by. "We'll all be ready for bed soon."

"Good luck gettin' your daddy up, chickadees. He's gonna stay till the bitter end."

"I'll take care of him," Lang said, voice an angry growl.

"Now, Lang, darlin'. Please don't make a scene. I can get him up. Neecy and Manual will help me."

"No, they won't. I'll do it. Least I can do after all you've been through."

Rose gave him a sharp look. "This has been a beautiful night. Let's not spoil it, please, Lang."

As the last guests headed out, Jaybo Dillon staggered their way, full glass in his hand. He dropped it on the dance floor, red wine splashing everywhere. Normally impeccably groomed, the elder Dillon's shirt was half untucked, his tie askew, and red wines stains trailed down the front of his white shirt.

"Jesus Christ," Lang muttered, heading toward him, leaving his mother to say the last goodbyes to friends. As he neared his father, Neecy and Manual appeared out of nowhere. They had obviously been watching their boss, ready to step in when needed.

Rose ran after her brother. "Leave him be, Lang! It will only make it worse if you get into it."

He shrugged out of her grasp and confronted his father, who was now propped on either side by a Rodriquez. "Hey, guys, I'll take over, thanks." He took the right side, which Neecy yielded. Her husband still held Jaybo Dillon under his left arm.

"Oh, boy, here we go," Jaybo said. "Back east big shot gonna step in and meddle where he's not wanted. Valley not good enough for you, and now you're back, thinking you can push everyone around. Well, we don't need you here!"

"Come on, Dad, let's get you to bed."

His father staggered and almost fell. Lang looked over his father's shoulder and met Manual's eyes. By tacit agreement, the latter stayed at his post.

Jaybo lashed out, swinging first at his son, then Manual. As the two men dragged him out the side door, Lang repressed an urge to pause and knock him cold. Mercifully, all but a few guests had departed, so the only witnesses to their slow, raucous exit were the caterers and ranch staff.

His father was heavy. He continued to shout and swear at the world and his son as Martha and Rose followed, both in tears.

When they got to the house, Jaybo seemed to get a second wind, and he stood straighter, shrugged out of their grasp, and shoved Lang. "Get the hell away from me, boy."

In deference to his mother and sister, Lang repressed the "fuck you," on his lips and said as calmly as possible, "Come on, Dad. Time for bed. You're upsetting Mom and Rosie."

"As if you care about them or anything here!" Unseeing eyes focused intermittently as Jaybo lashed out, first at his son, then Manual, knocking the latter down, ripping his jacket, and sending a tray of dirty glassware crashing to the floor. Several members of the catering staff stepped back to stare.

"That's it," Lang said. "We're not dragging him up the stairs. Manual, are you okay?"

"Yes, sir."

"You," Lang said to one of the bartenders who had just stepped in with a tray full of glasses. "Can you give us a hand?"

The young twentysomething man, with a blond crew cut and a broad, beefy frame, hesitated and glanced over at his boss, who nodded her approval. "Yes, of course, Dennis, help them for goodness' sake."

"Good. Okay, guys. We're gonna dump him in his study."

"Oh, no, you don't, you little twit!" Jaybo stood straighter and shook himself free. "I'm sleeping in my own bed tonight, and my bride's comin' with me." Unsteadily, he strode the length of the kitchen and flung open the door to the front hall. They all followed, with Martha slipping in front of the men and taking her husband's arm as they started up the stairs. His arm circled round her shoulders, and they made it to the top without a word.

As they reached Jaybo's bedroom, Lang grasped his mother's free hand. "Mom, let me. You go to bed."

"We'll be fine, darlin', don't worry. You and your sister go to bed. Thank you for a lovely evening."

"But?"

"No, Lang, no." Her eyes pleaded with him as the couple stepped inside and she closed the door.

Rose touched his shoulder. "Come on, let's go down and leave them be. She'll be okay. She'll flop him into bed, then head through to her room."

"Jesus Christ, what a nightmare," he said as he turned and followed Rose downstairs.

They met Neecy and Manual in the front hall. Both averted their eyes, ashamed for them and the household. "Can I bring you anything?" Neecy asked. "Coffee or something stronger?"

Lang smiled at her. "Thanks, Neecy. I'd kill for a tall seltzer water with lime."

"That sounds lovely," Rose said. "Me, too. We thought we might sit on the porch. You two are welcome to join us."

"Thanks, but we'd better stick to our cleanup right now," Neecy said as the two disappeared into the kitchen and the siblings headed for the front porch.

Lang took a deep breath and leaned back in the rocker to gaze at the blaze of stars overhead. "She's not ever gonna leave him, is she?"

"No," Rose said softly. "She loves him. He's her whole life."

"She deserves better."

"Yes."

"Would it help for us to talk to her?"

"I think it makes it worse. She's embarrassed, you see."

"Screw embarrassment. That bastard could kill her. She's half his size."

"Neecy and Manual look after her."

"What about getting a counselor in?"

"Can you see Dad in marriage counseling?"

"I don't mean for them. I mean getting someone for Mom. An abuse counselor who can help her break away."

"She won't do it, Lang. We tried after he broke her jaw. The hospital brought someone in. She went to a few sessions, insisted everything was fine, and never went again."

"Well, I'm not leaving until I know she's protected."

"That's good news. You're moving back for good, then?"

"Ha, ha. I'm on the road soon, come hell or high water. I will talk to him and if I have to, I'll hire a bodyguard for Mom."

"Don't be ridiculous."

"Just at night."

Rose shrugged and sipped her seltzer as she gazed out into the night. "What about Beth? Will it be hard to say goodbye to her?"

"We're just friends, for the hundredth time."

"Hey, right, and I'm flying to the moon in an hour."

"It's complicated."

"Love often is."

"I loved Cilla. Thought we'd be together forever, you know? We fit. Then we didn't. I don't trust myself in the love business anymore."

"What a load of horseshit. I always thought my big brother was smarter than that."

"I care about her, Rosie, I really do. And we have chemistry up the wazoo, if you get my drift. But she's a mess after her breakup, and I live three thousand miles away and may still be licking my wounds from Cilla."

"So why not at least see where it leads?"

Tired of talking about his love life, he looked over at her. "Is that what you're planning to do with Sam Morgan?"

"Very funny."

"Talk about chemistry. The man was all over you."

"Was not. Besides, I'm not his type."

"Which is?"

"I'm just boring, you know, and he tends to fall for interesting women."

"Now who's talking a load of horseshit! You're the least boring woman I know. You're accomplished, funny, smart, beautiful."

"Mousy, shy, unstylish."

"Baloney. Any man would be lucky to be with you."

"Stars are pretty tonight," she said, reaching across to take his hand.

"Yup."

CHAPTER 35

"Wasn't that a grand party the kids threw for Martha and Jay?" Leonora said, pleased to be presiding over the full table with her husband, three of her sons, and both daughters.

"Very nice," her husband said, winking at her from the far end of the table.

"Hope they got him to bed okay," Robbie said, forking several more pancakes from one of two platters in the middle of the table. "Old Jaybo was pretty smashed."

"Old Jaybo is always smashed after five o'clock," Ruthie said, waving her orange juice glass.

"Now, now, let's not indulge in idle gossip."

"Mom, it's just us," Beth said quietly. "Mr. Dillon's been a drunk for many years. It's certainly no secret."

Leonora stared at her older daughter, who rarely interjected comments or opinions during these kinds of conversations. "Are you feeling alright, Bethie?"

Beth ignored her mother's question and turned her attention to Carmela's amazing buttermilk pancakes. Truth was, she did not feel at all well. *Unbalanced* would be the best description.

"Yeah," Kyle said, peering over at his sister. "How 'bout Sampson showing up last night? How was that?"

Ben Senior saw his daughter's face blanch and eyed his son. "Leave her be, Kyle. That goes for the rest of you, too."

"Okay," Robbie said. "Can't we at least ask Ruthie about a certain cowboy whom she was lookin' really friendly with most of the night?"

"No, you cannot," Ruthie said, glaring at him. "Harley and I are friends and coworkers."

"Yeah, and I'm John Wayne," Sam said, grinning from ear to ear.

"John Wayne never indulged in gossip," Leonora said, giving her second son the eye.

Oh, for goodness' sakes, Beth thought. *This is why people don't have large families anymore!* She took her last bite of pancake and set her blue calico napkin aside. "This was great, Mom, but I've gotta run."

"Where?"

"I have a bunch of errands, and want to stop by the farm later." She stooped to kiss Sam and Robbie goodbye. Kyle was staying for the week, until after the fair, and both the others had promised to return.

"But, I thought…?" her mother said.

"Leave her be, Nora."

Ben Senior winked at his oldest daughter. Beth hugged him and hurried out, forestalling any further questions. Midway through breakfast, she had made a decision. She went up to her room, grabbed her cell phone, and punched in Lang's number before she could chicken out.

He answered immediately. "Hey, good morning."

"Hello. Great party last night. Hope cleanup wasn't too bad."

"That's where magical people like caterers come in, and, of course, Neecy, Manual, and the crew."

"Wasn't Jon involved in any of the party prep?" She referred to the Dillons' cook, Jon Wilson, who had been noticeably absent the previous evening.

"He doesn't do parties. He took the weekend off and went back to Laguna to see friends. How're you doing?"

A simple question, fraught with layers of meaning that Beth decided were best left unexcavated. "Fine. I was calling—I mean, I wondered—if you were busy later on today? I mean, if you are, there's no problem and I—"

Lang smiled, wishing they were speaking in person so he could take her in his arms draw her close, kissing her nervousness away. "Not busy at all. What'dya have in mind?"

"I thought I could ask Carmela to pack a picnic and we could take a ride?"

"I've only been riding the once with Rose. Sure you want to be with a tenderfoot from Boston?"

Beth laughed, happy for the first time since she woke up. "I'll take the risk. Would four-thirty or five suit you? We can meet behind Maggie and Ben's? That's about halfway. Unless you want to come here and ride one of our horses?"

"Four thirty is perfect. I'll be there, trying to stay in the saddle. Why don't I bring drinks or something? We have a shitload of food over here."

"Drinks would be great. See you then?"

"Absolutely."

Lang hung up, grinning from ear to ear. The prospect of a picnic with Beth made the conversation ahead with his father a little less daunting. As it turned out, their talk had to wait. The elder Dillon had risen early and disappeared, supposedly on winery business. He was still not back when Lang packed a saddle bag with wine and a thermos of lemonade, said goodbye to Rosie, and headed for the stable.

CHAPTER 36

They rode along the streambed, skirting the Morgan's Run stables and heading up into the hills. Beth watched Lang's lanky, strong frame as he sat very comfortably astride Jaybo Dillon's gorgeous chocolate morgan, Dandy. Tenderfoot indeed. Horse and rider moved as one as they climbed the south rise.

"I believe you were fibbing a bit, Lang Dillon. You look like you're ready for the rodeo."

"That's a hoot," he called over his shoulder, not daring to look back for fear of sliding off and over the cliff.

"Well, you're certainly more comfortable in the saddle than I am."

The day had been brutally hot, but now, in late afternoon, cool breezes wafted over them. As they reached the top of the rise, magnificent views of the farm and verdant valley stretched south and west to the mountains beyond.

"I'd forgotten how beautiful it is out here."

She nodded, bringing her horse up beside him. "It sure is. I try never to take it for granted. I always love the drive from brown, dusty Tucson, over the mountains to this." Unlike her siblings, Beth had never wanted a horse of her own. Today, she rode Tara, one of the ranch's gentle sorrel morgans. She reached forward and patted the horse's neck, whispering, "Good girl."

Lang gazed over at her. For the first time since he met her, Beth looked at peace. She wore faded jeans, a gray farm tee shirt, and a light beige canvas jacket, which she now had removed and tied round her waist. Her hair was tied back in loose braids, and strands framed her lovely face. "What do you think? We've been riding for a while. Wanta stop?"

"I think if we go a little further, there's a nice spot for a picnic. Did you ever come this way as kids, to the swinging tree?"

Lang shook his head. "Don't think so, but maybe."

"It's not much farther. Shall we shoot for that?"

"Lead the way, m'lady." He reined Dandy back to let Tara pass by as they took the trail bordering the high meadows to the west. Often those meadows were dotted with sheep, but now the sheep grazed nearer the farm, and the fields were deserted save the tall grasses and wildflowers. Green and verdant, the meadows stretched as far as the eye could see to the mountains dotted with thousands of saguaro cactuses and scrub.

Finally, Beth pointed ahead to a towering desert willow that stood at the edge of the meadow. "What do you think?"

"Looks perfect to me, but where's the swing?"

She laughed. "Long gone, but we're gonna have to hang another once Emma gets ready to ride the trails. She'll go crazy out here."

"She's a sweetheart," he said, alighting and coming to help her down.

Beth smiled, "Yes, she is."

While she was perfectly capable of dismounting on her own, Beth reached down and grasped his shoulder. As Lang gently took hold of her waist, she realized she was holding her breath and let it out in a whoosh. *Oh, my, here we go.*

Then they stood beside each other, each still holding on. "Hungry?" she asked.

"Starving."

Beth was reluctant to let go and knew that with the slightest encouragement, he would draw her closer. Shyly she gazed up into his beautiful blue eyes, which held hers. "I'm glad we decided to do this."

"Me, too." His smile melted her heart, and her knees shook. One gentle hand reached up and cupped her cheek. "Beth, I'm going to let you take the lead here. We won't do a thing unless you want to, unless you're ready. Okay?"

In answer, she drew him closer and reached up on tiptoes to kiss him. The kiss grew deeper as their lips parted and each delved and teased. Lang lifted her, gently cupping a breast with one hand as she ran her fingers through his hair. "Would you make love to me?" she whispered. "Please?"

Her words threatened to send him over the edge. He answered huskily, "You honor me with your request, Beth Morgan, and you have to know, I'd like nothing better."

"There's a blanket," she said breathlessly, pointing to Tara.

"I see it," he replied, reaching back with one hand to pull the patchwork quilt down and throw it to the ground. Miraculously it spread out with only one corner folded over, plenty of room for them to lie down.

As he trailed kisses along her neck, Lang gently unclasped her bra and in one fluid motion lifted it and her tee shirt over her head. Her eyes were open, taking in his every motion, breathless yet serene. She began unbuttoning his shirt, which he threw off, allowing her access to his lean, chiseled chest. Her hands, then her lips moved down, slowly tracing a trail to his jeans. He was rock hard, his manhood pressed against her body. Her hands caressed him, growing bolder and less gentle as they moved together.

"You're going to send me straight over the edge, Beth Morgan," he said, fingers moving down to unbutton her jeans. She laughed and kicked out of her boots, all the while caressing and rubbing, kissing him everywhere.

After both had slipped out of jeans and underclothes, he lifted her, placing her gently down on the quilt. "Is it okay if I make love to you everywhere, sweetheart?"

Beth nodded, too choked up and breathless to speak.

"Relax," he said, kissing her deeply, then trailing kisses down her neck, teasing and sucking at her nipples, then moving lower to her belly. His warm hands parted her legs, and he slipped fingers inside her warm wetness. "You're ready for me, aren't you, darlin'?"

She nodded, expected him to slip on the condom and plunge into her. Instead, his lips and tongue soon traveled down to replace his fingers as he licked, sucked, and teased her, finding her most sensitive places as he brought her to crashing, blinding climax. "Oh, oh, oh," she cried, serenity gone in the heat of her ecstasy.

He leaned back, gazing down at her. "Again?"

Beth shook her head, and her arms reached up and circled his neck. "I want you inside me, Lang Dillon, now. Please, please, please."

He grinned, thinking she had never looked more beautiful. "Your wish is my command, m'lady."

As he leaned down and kissed her deeply, Lang slipped on the condom and plunged into her. *Home,* he thought. *I'm home for the first time in my life.* It was the last coherent thought he had as they thrust together, a gentle rhythmic coupling that reached deeper and deeper until they moved as one. "Oh, Beth, oh, Beth," he moaned, losing what sanity remained as they reached a thundering climax together.

Afterwards, Lang rolled to his side, careful to hold her tightly, staying inside her, never wanting to let her go. She was smiling, tears in her eyes. "Sweetheart, are you okay?" She nodded and he kissed her nose, then each eye, hoping to dry her tears.

They lay in the warmth of each other's arms for a long time until he said, "I don't ever want to let you go."

She brushed hair from his forehead and gave him a lopsided grin. "You mean they'll find us here, starved to death, but never parted?"

"There are worse ways to go." He nuzzled her neck, sending shivers down her back.

"Hmm," she said, hand moving down his side to his hard, lean buttocks. As she did, she felt him harden inside her. "Think that condom's still intact?"

"Absolutely," he said, pulling her closer, thrusting gently at first as she joined him, their journey to climax slower at first, then reaching a crescendo that obliterated all thought save their urgent, insatiable need for each other.

This time, they fell asleep and woke as the sun was beginning to set. Beth stirred first and shivered, her back exposed to the cool evening air. "Hey," she whispered, nuzzling his neck.

He gave her a sleepy grin, then woke fully. "Oh, darling, you're freezing. Here." He slipped out of her and wrapped the quilt around her as both began rummaging around for their clothes.

When fully dressed, they smoothed out the quilt, grabbed the food and drink, and settled beside each other, suddenly shy and awkward.

"Wine, my dear?" Lang asked as he unwrapped two glasses and uncorked a pinot noir.

Beth nodded, taking sandwiches out of the saddle bag, thinking she felt more relaxed and happy than she had in a very long time. Maybe things had gone sour with Bill long before she found Skyler Blake in her bed?

CHAPTER 37

Lang took a bite of a portabella baguette, and a drop of Carmela's special sauce dripped down his chin. "Oh, my God, this is sinful, it's so good."

Beth laughed and waved half a chicken salad on sourdough at him. "Carmela created that sandwich and that sauce especially for Ben. He's been a vegetarian since he was a teenager. Truth be told, when he's around, she makes practically everything with him in mind. He's her favorite, he and my dad. Drives my mother crazy."

"More wine?"

"No, thanks. It's wonderful, but that glass went straight to my head. We have a half hour ride in the semidarkness ahead of us. I'm thinking maybe we should bring both horses to Morgan's Run and I'll drive you home. Maybe head out in about twenty minutes?"

"Can we talk a little first?"

"Of course. I'm sorry for my craziness the past week. This is not me at all. In fact, *this* is not me, either." She waved her arm, indicating the blanket and their lovemaking.

He laughed, corking the wine and filling his empty glass with lemonade. "Believe it or not, it's not me, either."

"So where does that leave us? Two crazy people who have lost touch with who they are?" Her eyes met his, waiting for an answer.

Lang reached over and caressed her chin. "What if this *is* who we are? What if we've been sleepwalking our entire lives till now? What if we've finally found out who we are together?"

"Is that what you think?"

"I don't know." He looked away, gazing down the valley as the sun sank lower. "I don't seem to be able to get my head clear about anything out here."

"But you think when you get home, you will be?"

"Maybe. Who knows? My father drives me crazy, I'm worried about our mom, and I've started an intense, passionate relationship with an incredible woman I'd dearly love to know better."

"Well, I may be a mess, but I do know one thing. I love you, Lang Dillon. I don't expect you to return the sentiment, so don't start cowering like a scared jackrabbit."

"Do I look like I'm cowering?"

He moved closer and placed his hand on her thigh. She laughed and moved out of his grasp. "Oh, no, you don't. It's gonna be dark soon."

Beth started to stand, and he held her wrist. "Beth, I know I can't give you the answer you want and deserve. I have very strong feelings for you, but I—"

A call in the distance startled them, and Beth looked north, surprised to see her eldest brother galloping toward them. Flustered, she feared Ben was coming to defend her honor. Hands on hips, she stood as he neared them, astride on his sorrel quarter horse, Rowdy. Lang sprang up and was standing beside her by the time Ben reached them.

"What are you doing up here?" she said, eyes searching her brother's. He didn't look angry or belligerent. He looked frightened.

"Something's happened," he said, turning to Lang. "Your dad…they found him unconscious in the winery office. He's been taken to Valley Hospital. Rose and your mom are with him."

Lang stared at him in shock. "Do they know what happened? Is he…?"

"He's stable. They think it was his heart, but they're running tests. Rose asked me to find you."

Beth turned to him. "Go with Ben. I'll clean this up and follow you down. He'll take you to the hospital."

Ben jumped down and threw their supplies into saddlebags, the blanket over his shoulder. "No one's staying behind. We're all set. Let's go." He helped her onto Tara as Lang grabbed Dandy's mane and leapt astride him.

They galloped across the meadow, then slowed to head down the trail that ran along the eastern slope, the quickest way back to the Morgan's Run stables. When they reached the stables, Beth dismounted and said to Lang, "Go. I'll take care of this. Jeb's here. He can help me."

In the growing darkness, Ben and Lang hopped into the jeep. Beth watched the lights of the Rover as they disappeared, then turned to help Jeb Barnes, Maggie's assistant, take the horses in.

CHAPTER 38

"Oh, Lang, thank God," Rose said, stepping out of the intensive care room to hug her brother.

Lang could see his father through the glass, connected to tubes, wires, and a breathing apparatus. Martha Dillon sat beside him, holding his hand.

"What the hell happened?"

"Another heart episode. They're still running tests. Manual found him when he went to close up. We don't know how long he'd been lying there."

"Has he spoken to anyone?"

"No, he's been unconscious the whole time, although Mom swears he's been squeezing her hand."

"Jesus Christ," he said, sinking down into a molded plastic chair just outside the room.

"Are you okay?" she asked, sitting down beside him. "You look a little green."

Before Lang could answer, a tall doctor with a hooked nose and a shock of gray hair greeted them. "Are you Mr. Dillon's relatives?"

"Yes, his son and daughter," Rose said, waving to her mother, who hurried out to join them.

"I'm Dr. Matthias," he said, leading them into a small anteroom. "We can talk in here."

Once inside, he closed the door and motioned them to the sofa and chairs, then pulled one of the molded plastic chairs and sat facing them. "I've read through your husband's charts," he said, gazing at Martha, eyes solemn. "Mr.

Dillon has had a more significant heart attack than the one he experienced last year. He has several major blockages that must be corrected. His cardiologist, Dr. Richmond, is away until the end of next week, but I've spoken with him. He feels we should operate immediately."

"What if we choose to wait for Harold?" Martha asked. "He knows Jay so well, and we've been with him for years."

"We're giving your husband large doses of blood thinners and medications to ease the blockages, but they do not remove them. As long as they are present, Mr. Dillon is not getting adequate oxygen to his brain and the rest of his body. He's at grave risk of another episode at any time."

"What would the procedure entail?"

"We would put in four stents to correct the blockages and monitor him closely. It's risky because his liver is damaged by the cirrhosis and last year's flare-up of esophageal varices caused by the cirrhosis."

"Cirrhosis!" Lang said, staring at his mother. "When did this start?"

"Now, Lang, settle down. Your dad didn't want to worry you kids."

"Did you know, Rosie?"

His sister shook her head.

Dr. Matthias looked from one to the other. "Would you like a few minutes to discuss all this, and I'll come back?"

"Absolutely not!" Martha Dillon said, sitting up straighter, taking hold of her daughter's hand. "We want him to have the treatment he needs as soon as possible."

"Sorry," Lang said. "She's right, of course. Stents? Those don't involve open heart surgery, do they?"

"No, we'll go in through veins in his groin. There is a greater risk with your father's history of bleeding, but if we don't do the procedure, he has no chance."

"When do you want to operate?" Rose asked quietly.

"Immediately, with the family's consent."

"I'm a physician, a pediatric surgeon. I would like to observe from the gallery, if I may."

"That's not a good idea, Dr. Dillon, but it's your choice."

"I would like to be there."

He nodded, expression grave. "I'll have one of the nurses come for you when it's time."

"Thank you," she said softly.

"Have you got any questions for me?" Dr. Matthias asked, gazing from one to the other. They shook their heads in response, and he rose. "I'll be off, then. I'll come back and talk with you after the procedure."

After returning their mother to Jaybo's bedside, Lang and Rose walked the corridor, talking softly. Finally he said, "This is gonna be a long night. I think we can use some coffee. I'll run down. You wait in case they call you."

Rose nodded, tears in her eyes, as she watched him walk away.

CHAPTER 39

When Lang returned with the coffee, Rose had gone to the observation theater, and Beth was there with her parents. Leonora went to sit with Martha and Beth sat beside Lang, holding his hand. Sometimes one dozed and rested a head on the other's shoulder.

While his wife and Martha dozed in chairs by the bed, Ben Senior slept in a recliner just inside Jaybo's room. Thus, he was the most rested one when Rose appeared shortly after six a.m., her face grim, even though she gave them a thumbs-up. "Dr. Matthias will be down shortly," she said softly, coming to sit beside her brother. Ben Senior, Martha, and Leonora woke simultaneously and came out to the hall to join them.

With dark circles under his piercing gray eyes, Dr. Matthias soon appeared and pulled up a chair in front of them. "Well, he made it. He's weak, but he came through it okay. We've got him heavily sedated right now so he can rest. He'll be in recovery for at least four hours. Then we'll bring him back here. You might want to go home and get some rest. Come back midafternoon when he should be awake."

Martha Dillon burst into tears and buried her head in her hands as Leonora patted her shoulder.

"This is good news, Mom" Rose said, but her tone was neither confident nor optimistic.

Dr. Matthias answered their questions, then departed, assuring them that he would be checking in every few hours and that "Mr. Dillon is getting the best of care."

Yeah, right, Lang thought. *What remotely competent doctor practices medicine at this rinky dink hospital?* His sister was clearly worried, and he wondered if he should suggest their father be moved to Phoenix or Tucson. *Later,* he thought, squeezing his mother's hand. Not that he didn't appreciate the Morgans' presence, especially Beth's, but what ICU allowed anyone off the street to waltz right in? Were there any protocols or procedures at all?

After a short conversation, Beth stood up. "Why don't we take Dr. Matthias's advice and go home and rest? We have Mom's car, and I have the truck. Between us, we can get everyone home."

Rose stood up. "I'll take a ride, at least to get a change of clothes. Thanks, Beth."

"I'll stay," Lang said quietly.

Surprised, his sister stared at him.

"It's fine," he said. "I think you and Mom should go home. I'll hang around until one or both of you get back. Then I'll take a break."

As the day went on, Jaybo Dillon's condition improved, and he was moved back to his room. They each took turns sitting with him, even though he barely acknowledged their presence. Lang had been there when they wheeled Jaybo up. All his father said was, "You're here," then lapsed into unconsciousness again. Lang went home and showered, returning in the early evening to relieve his mother and sister. By then, the father had woken and was able to manage talk, albeit briefly, as he moved between sleep and wakefulness.

At ten p.m., Lang looked over at his mother and sister. "You two go home. I had a rest. I'll stay. That recliner looks pretty good right about now."

Rose watched, trying to read his mood. "There's really no need. The nurses say he'll probably sleep all night, and they'll call us if there's any change."

"I'll be fine. Go."

He hugged them both before walking them to the car. When he returned, he grabbed a bottle of water, chips, and a turkey sandwich from the cooler Neecy had sent and came to sit by his father. He had just taken a bite when she walked into the room.

CHAPTER 40

"Cilla? What are you doing here? How did you…?" He stood as she approached. She was lovely as always in leggings, boots, and a stylish leather jacket in soft coffee, her long chestnut hair falling over her thin shoulders.

"Relax, sweetie. I spoke to Neecy." She hugged him and kissed him on the cheek.

"She called you?"

"No, I phoned the house last night wanting to speak to you, and she told me. I hopped on the first plane."

"Why?"

"What kind of a question is that, sweetie? I wanted to be here for you, of course. How's your mom holding up?"

Martha Dillon had never warmed to Cilla, but his father had adored her. Lang was glad he was asleep. Her appearance probably would have given him another heart attack.

"She's fine," he said warily, pointing to the hallway.

When they were seated, he said, "What's going on, Cilla? We haven't seen each other for what, eight or nine months? You're about to marry what's-his-name, and now you want to be here for me?"

"Brent and I are taking a breather."

"So?"

"So I wanted to talk to you, see how you were doing. I miss you." Her brilliant green eyes pleaded. Cilla could always wrap him round her little finger with one glance.

Lang hated to admit it, but at that moment, there was something soothing about sitting beside her. Raw after the past week and the past twenty-four hours, he found the presence of someone from his real life comforting. Cilla wasn't a part of this alien land. She came from the land of the sane, a civilized place that had shaped him more than the Valley. He nodded and whispered, "Thanks," taking her hand in his.

At that moment, Beth came through the double doors, Rose at her side. The tender scene was not lost on either of them.

Rose and Cilla had been friendly during the years they had been together, but the two women had lost touch since the breakup. She would never have called Cilla about her dad.

"Cilla!" she cried as she stepped forward to hug her.

Beth stood still, watching the three, wishing she could fade into the woodwork.

Mortified, Lang hopped up and came to her side. "Beth, hi. Thanks for coming back."

She nodded. "Looks like you're busy. I'll get out of your hair. How's he doing?"

"Fine. He's doing fine. Sleeping. Stay if you want."

"Thanks, but I think I'll take off."

Beth took a step back as Cilla came forward, not missing a nuance in their interaction. *So this is the competition,* she thought, extending her hand. "Pricilla Beatty. Hello. Always nice to meet one of Lang's hometown friends."

Neecy has a big mouth, Lang thought, watching Cilla. Like their father, Neecy had adored his college girlfriend and had no doubt given her an earful about the past week and his attraction to Beth Morgan. *That's why she's here. Cilla loves a good fight, especially since she rarely loses. She loves Dad, but this is about her not wanting to be replaced now that Mr. Hedge Fund has gone south.*

As Beth shook the other woman's hand, she caught Rose's eye. Lang's sister looked stricken. "Hello, what a surprise. I'll just head out and let you all catch up." She turned to Lang and Rose. "I'm so glad he's doing well. Please let us know if you need anything. Could we have Carmela make up some food?"

"Thanks, Beth," Rose said. "We'll let you know. Jon comes back tonight, so between him and Neecy, we should be all set."

"Well, don't hesitate," Beth said, addressing all of her remarks to Rose. "Nice to meet you, Ms. Beatty."

Cilla beamed and waved slender arms. "Absolutely! Hope to see more of you during my stay."

"Here, I'll walk you out," Lang said, moving to accompany her.

"No need, thanks. Stay with Rose and your dad. Take care."

Beth turned and practically ran out of the ICU. As she pushed through the double doors, she overheard Cilla saying, "Oh, Rosie, so good to see you, even under these circumstances! Let's catch up."

Beth did not wait to hear Rose's reply.

CHAPTER 41

The next two days were a blur as they worked to arrange caregivers for Jaybo. The doctors refused to release him without nursing care, so an agency had lined up help for at least four weeks. Cilla was staying at the house and Lang had to admit, she was a huge help. A world-class organizer, she fit right into the household routines. Rose commuted back and forth from Tucson, and in between helping his mother and visiting his father, Lang tried to keep up with work as projects and responsibilities mounted.

He tried to phone Beth several times each day, but she never picked up. Finally, he decided that with everything else going on, it might be kindest to leave her alone. He had no intention of rekindling anything with Cilla, who, when not helping with her father's care arrangements, spent her days gossiping with Neecy or talking on the phone. Several times he had overheard what sounded like a heated conversation, and he suspected that things with Brent were far from over.

Lang had offered to stay longer, for his mother's sake, but she insisted that he go. Even though Martha Dillon wanted her son to stay more than anything in the world, she knew that he needed to go home. He did, however, move his departure date from Thursday to Friday.

*****

"Leave her be, Nora," Ben Senior said, hand on his wife's as she moved to stop Beth. "She knows what she's doing."

It was Wednesday morning, and Beth was headed to the farm for a few hours, then into Tucson for lunch with Bill. Her mother did not approve and had been trying to persuade her to let their attorney handle the transfer or sale of the condo.

"She's still so fragile. I wish she'd let Arthur handle things. His office is two blocks from the condo, for goodness' sakes."

"This is Beth we're talkin' about, honey. She's the strongest of all our children."

"Not true! That's just a façade. In matters of the heart, she's a marshmallow."

He smiled, gazing at Leonora with affection. "What do we know about love, honey? We've been head over heels for over forty years."

"Pish tush! That's right, we know a lot about love at our age, and I know if you'd done what Bill Sampson did, I'd never be able to be in the same town as you, never mind the same room. And I certainly would not be running down to Tucson to have lunch! I'd be at home, arranging a tarring and feathering!"

He chuckled and rose, bending to kiss the top of her head. "Lucky thing for me that I've only had eyes for you, darlin'. Gotta go. Group comin' in this morning."

"The rodeo people? I though they weren't coming till Friday."

"Nope, they're comin' for a few days R & R, spa treatment, fair, then out on the trail with Ben and Harley for four nights."

Leonora grinned, forgetting her distress over Beth. "They have kids, don't they?"

"Yep, four or five, I think."

"Are they all going on the trail ride?"

"Yep, they're older, I think. Littlest is maybe eight or nine."

"I'd give big money to see Harley Langdon trying to corral a bunch of eight-year-olds on the Switchback Trail."

"What about our son?" he asked, chuckling. "Emma's hardly your typical kid, so he hasn't had much experience, either."

"I imagine there'll be some stories to tell," she said, kissing his cheek. "Won't be long after that, you and I will be packing to take off."

"Now, about that, Nora."

Her hand shot up. "Ben Morgan, don't you dare bring up the subject of postponing our trip! We are going, and that's that." With those words, Leonora disappeared into the kitchen.

*****

After overseeing the unloading of gear and equipment and checking on the day's harvest, Beth headed back to the farm office, washed up, and changed her clothes. She and Bill were meeting at a café near the university, a place he had suggested. She had never been there. With a lump in her throat, she headed out. She had borrowed Ruthie's jeep since it was much easier to park than her truck. As she pulled into a space, she spied Bill crossing the street and waved.

The lump in her throat felt bigger as she sat across from him, placing her hands gently on the white tablecloth in front of her. He looked more rested. The circles under his eyes were less pronounced. Beth forced a smile. "How are you?"

He shrugged. "I guess the words are *saddened, but resigned*. You?"

"About the same."

He picked up the menu. "Would you like wine?"

"No, thanks. You should have told me this was a bit upscale. I'm not really dressed for it."

"You look lovely, as you always do, Beth." He loosened his tie and pushed his glasses up his nose, gazing downward. "Everything's good, so order anything you like. My treat."

"That's not necessary."

"Please, Beth, let me at least buy you lunch."

"Of course. Thank you."

Samuel, the waiter, appeared, and she ordered the quiche special with a salad. Bill ordered a cobb salad. "Can I get you something to drink besides water, folks?" Short and dark-haired, dressed in black slacks and a starched white dress shirt, Samuel looked about ten.

"Iced tea for me," she said.

"Me, too. That'd be great," Bill said, handing him both the menus.

When the waiter disappeared, he said, "So, here we are."

"Yes."

"I don't suppose you've changed your thinking about us?"

"No, I'm sorry." Beth gazed at him, full of sadness. She would miss him. She already did miss him. Terribly. The touch of his warm shoulder as she slipped into bed, their quiet dinners, each sharing the ups and downs of the day, watching a silly television show, going to a movie or the theater, hiking, laughing, dancing and singing at concerts in the university fieldhouse. The life they had had was precious and irreplaceable, she thought, slowly spreading her napkin across her knees.

"I'm sorry, too. I love you very much, Beth Morgan. I will always love you."

"Yes, I suppose that's true for both of us."

"Then what the hell are we doing here?"

Samuel served the teas and hastened away.

"Beth, if we both still love each other, then why can't we go home, hire a good therapist, and get through this?"

"Please don't start. I can't, Bill. That's all. I still love you, I do, but I can't go back, or go forward with us. I just can't."

They said nothing for several minutes as Bill reached down and rifled through his briefcase. Samuel brought their food, refilled their teas, and retreated, the couple's silence full of unspoken warning.

Bill slipped a folder out of his case and set it on the table beside his salad. "I've got all the paperwork, I think. If you're not coming back, I don't want the condo. If you don't want it, we'll sell. I've gotten an estimate from a realtor, and she actually may have a buyer. It's appreciated in value quite a bit, almost double what we paid for it."

She nodded, completely uninterested in the condo's value or anything about it. "Will we need an attorney for any of this?"

"Maybe. Phil Rubinstein at the college is happy to help. He'll do it for nothing."

"Are you sure? My parents' lawyer, Arthur Stokes, could also take care of things."

"There's no need. And we sure don't need to pay Stokes's exorbitant fees."

"I expect he'd do it for nothing, but Phil is fine, too. Whatever you want."

"It's very straightforward. I'm giving it to you. All of it, so once the sale goes through, I'll have Phil cut the check."

"Absolutely not. We bought it together. It should be split fifty-fifty."

"Not in Arizona. Moral turpitude carries a high price."

"Don't be ridiculous. That's only in divorce cases, and since we are not married, we will dissolve our partnership equitably."

"Please let me do this, Beth."

"No, and I won't hear another word about it. If Phil won't arrange the fifty-fifty split, I will ask Arthur to step in."

"As you wish."

"Thank you," she said, and reached over to take his hand. "I know you're trying to make up for everything, and I appreciate the gesture, but there's no need."

"Oh, God, Beth, what a stupid fool I was."

He looked so lost and scared. She gave him a slight smile, her heart aching. "I can't argue with that."

"Do you think you can ever forgive me?"

"Yes. I can't honestly say that I'm there yet, but I will try very hard, okay?" Her eyes blurred with unbidden tears, and she gazed down at her lap.

"Oh, darling, I'm sorry. I've made you cry. I'm so sorry. I can't ever remember you crying at any time when we were together."

"I've heard that a lot lately. I seem to be abnormally good at crying right now."

"I'm so sorry, Beth."

"I know. Let's finish our lunches and try to let things go for now, okay?"

"Do you think there might be a time someday when we could be friends?"

She smiled, dabbing her tears with her napkin. "I hope so."

*****

As she drove home, Beth realized that the lump in her throat was gone, and she felt calmer. Infinitely sad, but much calmer. In a day or so, Lang Dillon would be gone back to Boston, and she could begin the work of picking up the pieces of her shattered life. Maggie had recommended a therapist whom she said saved her life, and Beth decided to make an appointment for the following week. As she drove up the Gila, she remembered a week earlier, the day when her world had fallen apart and she had met Lang Dillon on the dusty road.

CHAPTER 42

As Rose drove through the winery gates, she felt irritable and wished she could head back to her Tucson condo. She had just come from Valley Hospital, visiting her dad, then checking with the staff about his discharge the following day. The hospital had found them nursing support, and a Ms. Partridge was scheduled to accompany him home and stay for the first three days and nights. She would rotate with either one or two other nurses the agency had lined up, depending upon how long they felt her father needed care.

Rose's irritation did not relate to her father or arrangements for his care. It was about the dinner ahead and her longing for the neat, quiet life she had made for herself in Tucson. Truth was, she had never cared for Cilla Beatty, and the past few days had not changed that opinion. Cilla had been fawning all over her brother, mother, and father and, of course, she and Neecy were thick as thieves. It did not appear that Jon Wilson, the cook, had fallen under her charms, and her mother seemed to avoid her as much as was polite. *No matter*, thought Rose, heading in with her overnight case. Cilla would be gone tomorrow, thank goodness.

*****

Jon outdid himself with shrimp and scallop shish kebabs, flavored with a piquant lime cilantro marinade. Served with saffron rice and a medley of field greens, the meal was light and delicious. Jon had brought the seafood back from his trip to the coast, and he suggested a crisp pinot grigio to accompany it.

"Jon, this wine is superb," Cilla said, gushing at the cook as he refilled her glass. "Is it from the vineyard?"

Suppressing a smirk, he refrained from explaining that these were not the conditions or climate for pinot grigio grapes, and simply said, "No, Ms. Beatty, I brought it back from my trip."

"Well, it's sublime, and I must write down the label and vintage."

Lang watched his former girlfriend, remembering for the hundredth time why they no longer fit. "So, Rosie, how was everything with dad?"

"Fine. They're all set for tomorrow. They expect the discharge will be completed by noon, and Ms. Partridge will ride out in the ambulance with him."

"So they still won't let me drive him home?" their mother asked.

Rose shook her head. "I think you should stay here and get everything ready for when he arrives."

"Neecy can do that. She's already made up Ms. Partridge's room and gotten Dad's things settled in the study."

"Neecy's taking Cilla to the airport, Mother, remember?"

"As I've told you," Cilla said, "that is absolutely unnecessary. I can hire a cab."

"No need," Lang said. "I'm sure Neece is looking forward to it." He gave his sister a conspiratorial look.

Rose studied her brother for a minute before saying, "Guess who I saw in town today? I was having lunch with colleagues in the back room of La Forge, and I spied Beth Morgan with Bill. They seemed like they were having a nice time. The food at La Forge is amazing. You feel as if you're in the middle of Paris instead of downtown Tucson."

Lang's face clouded over and he stared down at his plate. He was clearly furious, his mood obvious to all three women. His mother shook her head, rolling her eyes at her daughter.

Cilla paled, watching the man she had loved for so long, and knowing with certainty that he now loved someone else. *He might not know it,* she mused, watching Lang's jaw clench and unclench, *but he's crazy in love with that plain Jane Beth Morgan. Time for me to go home.*

Dinner over at last, Lang excused himself and tried for the twentieth time to phone Beth, but once again he reached her voice mail. Muttering under his breath, he slammed out of the house and took a long walk, not even caring if a snake or other creature crossed his path. By the time he returned, Cilla had gone to bed, as had his mother and sister.

Lang grabbed his cell. *You can not answer my calls all you want, Beth Morgan,* he thought as he headed for his room, *but one way or the other, I'm going to talk to you before I leave.*

CHAPTER 43

After a hasty breakfast, Cilla grabbed the last of her things, hugged Martha and Rose, then called to Neecy. Lang stowed her bags in the Rover and left the keys on the dashboard. "It's got a full tank, Neece, so you're all set."

When Cilla appeared, Neecy stepped back and hopped into the driver's seat, giving them some privacy.

"Well, this is it, darling," she said, reaching up to stroke his jaw. "It's been wonderful to see you again. Thank you for not kicking me out."

"Never. Thanks for all your help." He took her hand and kissed it lightly. "Have a good flight."

"And you, drive safe. You'll be home in a week or so, right?"

"Something like that. I've got a few stops along the way."

"Will be good to know you're back in Boston."

Ignoring her meaning, he said, "Good luck with Brent. Hope all the phone calls back and forth have smoothed things over for you guys."

She rolled her eyes. "Oh, Brent and I'll be fine. We'll either kill each other or get married before the year's out."

"I hope it's the latter, if that's what you want."

"Well, since I can't have you, I guess I'll have to settle for Brent and all his millions."

He chuckled. "That should more than compensate."

"Maybe." She stared at him, expression pensive. "And what about you? Are you leaving your heart here or dragging her back to Boston?"

"What're you talking about?"

"Oh, Lang, I've known you a long time, sweetheart. You never looked at me the way you look at Beth Morgan. I may be a lot of things, but I'm neither blind nor stupid. You shouldn't be, either."

"Better get going or you'll miss your flight. Goodbye, Cilla. Thanks for coming for Dad. It meant a lot to him, and me." He kissed her cool white cheek and hugged her.

"Love you, darling," she whispered. "Take care of yourself."

With those words, Cilla Beatty sashayed around the Rover and hopped in, knowing with certainty that it would be a very long time before she laid eyes on Lang Dillon again.

*****

An hour later, Lang pulled up to the Morgan's Run stables in one of the old, battered winery trucks. After postponing it several times, he had called over the previous day and made an appointment to talk with Maggie, Jeb, and maybe either Harley or Ben about riding equipment. As he got out of the truck, Maggie emerged from the barn and waved. "Hey, Lang. Good morning."

"Hey, Maggie. Is this a good time?"

"Absolutely! Jeb and I have a whole list of innovative ideas for you."

"What about the two other cowboys?" he asked, referring to Ben and Harley.

Maggie rolled her eyes. "They're all over the place, having fits with the upcoming trip, the fair, and the people who are checking in today. Don't worry, we have their list. You wouldn't want to see them today, believe me. Harley's about to combust, and my husband's in a mood."

"Oh?"

"He's fretting over leaving me next week in 'my condition.' She patted her stomach. "He seems to forget that I had Emma all on my own while working full-time. Come on, we can sit out back where it's shady. Want something to drink?"

An hour later, Lang had jotted down many ideas for general equipment needs, some of which sounded promising, especially the ideas Harley and Ben had given him about equipment for the pack trips. He was about to shut his notebook when

Maggie said, "Now that we've talked about needs around here, I'd like to chat a little about the camp. Do you know about our plans for the riding camp for handicapped kids?"

"A little, yes. Sounds amazing."

"It will be when we have everything we need to ensure the kids' safety. We want them to feel totally confident and comfortable on horseback. Some things I've researched and can get, but I'd like to run some ideas by you, if that's an area that might interest your company?"

Lang smiled and flipped his notebook open. "Absolutely. Shoot."

Maggie and Jeb spent another hour describing the challenges and needs of riders of differing ages and disabilities. While this would clearly be a challenge and a dramatic departure for Rambler Sports, Lang was more excited than he had been about any new product idea in a long time.

Finally, Jeb excused himself to make a run into town. "Want anything, Mags?" he asked. "I could get lunch?"

She smiled up at her handsome assistant. "Thanks, Jeb. I'm all set."

"Well, nice to see you again, Mr. Dillon. I hear you're taking off soon."

"Yup, that's the plan. Headed out Friday. Thanks so much for all your input, Jeb."

Jeb tipped his hat and turned away, headed into the barn.

"He's a great kid."

"Yes, he is." Maggie gazed at him for thirty seconds, then added, "Don't mind saying I'll be sad to see you go, Lang."

"Yeah, well, it's time, I guess."

"Have you spoken to Beth?"

He shook his head. "Won't take my calls."

"Perhaps she was waiting until your fiancée left."

"Cilla is not my fiancée. She's my ex-girlfriend. As in, we broke up last year. She left this morning."

"Oh."

"You might tell Beth that, if you see her."

Maggie smiled at him, taking a long sip of her lemonade. "I think I'll stay out of this one. Besides, you should tell her yourself."

"How?"

"I don't know, but please don't leave without saying goodbye. You'll regret it, and she'll be devastated."

"From what I hear, she's going back to Bill."

Maggie's eyes widened, and she set down her glass. "Who told you that?"

"Someone saw them in Tucson, having a cozy lunch at a fancy restaurant."

"That's all?"

"What more do you need?"

She was about to respond when Harley appeared, hat pushed back, a coil of rope in his hand. "Well, if it isn't love-'em-and-leave-'em Dillon."

"Don't start," Lang said.

"Look, I don't give a shit whether you stay or fly to the moon, but Beth Morgan is like a sister to me, and I don't like to see her mistreated."

Maggie glared at her boss. "Harley, why don't you get something to drink and cool off?"

"I'm plenty cool, thanks."

"Look, Langdon, I haven't mistreated Beth and never would."

"So what do you call throwing your girlfriend in her face when she was coming in to stay by your side?"

"Cilla is not my girlfriend. I had no idea she was coming. She just showed up."

"Why didn't you send her packing?"

Feeling tired and defeated, Lang shook his head. "It's complicated. Anyway, she's gone now."

"Whoop-de-doo," Harley said, staring down at Maggie. "Listen, I gotta go into town for a bit. Ben should be back soon." He turned to Lang. "And if I were you, Dillon, I'd hightail it outta here. If you think I'm pissed at you, you damn well don't want to see Maggie's husband."

"That's enough, Harley." Maggie scowled at him, but her boss had already turned heel and disappeared into the barn. "Pay no attention to him, Lang. He's a hot head. He's always like this before a pack trip, barking at everyone. Jeb and I have learned just to keep our heads down and stay out of his way."

"He's right, you know. I've been a world-class jerk to Beth. No wonder she's run back to Bill."

She reached out and grasped his arm. "Talk to her, please, Lang. Don't leave without at least saying goodbye."

"Thanks, Maggie," he said.

They both stood, and he gave her a hug. "Ben Morgan's a lucky man."

"I'm lucky, too," she said, smiling up at him, her dazzling blue eyes full of warmth.

"I'm gonna keep checking the camp website for updates."

"It's not up yet, but Sally, one of Mr. Morgan's administrative assistants at the main office is a computer whiz, and she's building it for us."

He handed her his card. "Please email and let me know when it goes live. Have you thought of what you'll call the camp?"

Maggie grinned, nodding. "It's called Emma's Dream."

CHAPTER 44

The sadness of her lunch with Bill resonated as Beth walked into therapist Haley Alverez's office for the first time Thursday morning. They spent their first session with Beth telling her story. Occasionally, Haley asked a question, but for the most part, Beth talked and Haley listened. As they said goodbye, the short, round woman in brightly colored caftan and waist-length silver hair gave her a hug. "It will get better, Beth. I promise. Time is a great healer."

"Everyone tells me that."

"Because it's true. You're still in shock right now. That's why your mouth is dry and you can't sleep or eat."

"What about the crying? Will it ever stop? Before last week, I hadn't cried since I was a child. It's not like me at all. I've come so unglued! I'm always the calm, steady one."

Haley squeezed her hand. "You can be calm and steady with tears. Crying at a time like this is actually cathartic and healthy."

"Lucky me," Beth said, wiping tears from her cheeks.

"I mean it, Beth. Let yourself cry. When you're alone and out of everyone's earshot, let yourself cry audibly, as loud as you can, as long as you need. It will help the anxiety and help you heal."

"Guess I'll have to saddle up and head out to the other end of the Valley."

"Good idea, but in a pinch, a closed car parked on its own is pretty soundproof and comfortable."

"We haven't talked about Lang much."

Haley studied her, trying perhaps to gauge whether to say more. "There's always next time."

"He leaves tomorrow."

"Yes, but Boston isn't the moon. There'll be time to talk when you're ready. Better not to push things until you are."

"I know your next patient is probably waiting, but after listening to me ramble on, do you think I threw myself into the thing with Lang on the rebound, as a way to run from the hurt of Bill?"

Haley smiled. "I don't know you well enough to say anything about that, but even when I do get to know you better, my answer will be the same. That's a question only you can answer, Beth. See you next Thursday?"

"So that's how therapy works? No advice, I guess? I talk, you listen, and I slowly figure things out."

Haley chuckled. "Something like that, but progress will come, I promise. I prefer to support my clients as they come up with the answers they are seeking."

"Thanks, Haley. See you next week."

As she parked at the farm, Beth had to admit she felt calmer than she had since the day she had discovered Bill and his lover. *That will have to be enough*, she thought, waving to Raoul as she headed in to find Ruthie.

*****

Lang headed out of Morgan's Run. He considered taking a detour to the farm, but he had promised to check in on his father, so headed to the winery instead. As he drove in, he spied the Rover parked at the house and Neecy just alighting.

"Hey!" she called.

"Hi, Neece. Thanks for the airport run."

"No problem. Gave Cilla and me time to catch up and say goodbye. She's such a sweetheart. We'll miss her. I'm sure you're excited to get back to Boston."

Ignoring the housekeeper's allusion, he said, "Listen, Neece, can you do me a favor and run this truck down to the winery? I'm gonna check on Dad. Then I've gotta go out."

"Course. Leave the key in it. I'll call Manual and see how soon they need it, then take it down."

She followed him into the house, where they found Martha Dillon fussing over her husband. The nurse, Judy Partridge, stood in the background in faded mauve scrubs, calm and watchful. Partridge appeared to be in her forties. Her short blond hair was covered with a net. She was short, compact and, Lang guessed, strong. He nodded to her.

When Martha spied her son and housekeeper, she visibly relaxed. "Oh, good. You two are back. Neecy, Jon's gone into town for groceries. Can you make us some lunch? What do you think, Judy?" she asked, turning to the nurse. "Would a turkey sandwich be okay for him?"

"Absolutely, if he's up to it." Judy looked across at Jaybo, who was propped up in his hospital bed, looking like a grand pooh-bah.

"Would you two hens stop talking about me like I'm not here? I'm perfectly capable of ordering whatever I want for lunch. Neecy, I'll take my turkey sandwich with lettuce, tomato, pickles, and plenty of mayo. And some chips and salsa and iced tea, too."

"Lang, sweetheart," his mother said. "Can Neecy fix you something?"

"Thanks, but I'm just checking in. Got some errands to run."

"Oh, but this is your last day, sweetie."

"And I'll be back in plenty of time to spend it with you guys."

"Good, because Jon's got a special dinner planned. Judy, would you like lunch, too?"

"Thanks, that would be lovely, but I can fix it myself."

"Nonsense. Neecy, three turkey sandwiches, no pickles for me, and iced teas. Thanks. Maybe Judy can come with you, in case she likes her sandwich a special way." She waved at the housekeeper and nurse, shooing them ahead of her into the kitchen.

Lang took a seat beside the bed. "How d'you feel, Dad?"

"Like crap."

"Guess that's to be expected."

"So, you're taking off tomorrow?"

"Yup. I asked Mom and Rose if they wanted me to stay, but they say they can manage."

"Course we can manage. What the hell do you think we've been doin' for the last fifteen years?"

"Of course." Lang spoke softly, working hard to control his temper. For his mother's sake, he did not want to provoke an argument. As he gazed at the petulant figure beside him, he felt strangely at peace. With glistening clarity, he realized he felt nothing for his father. Neither love nor hate, just tolerance. He would tolerate and respect his parent for the sake of his mother and sister, whom he genuinely loved.

"Look, son, I don't need your pity or your checking in. For your mother's sake, let's have a nice dinner tonight, then say our goodbyes."

Lang stood and watched the bravado fade from his father's face. He was scared to death, but working hard not to show it. "Works for me. Can I get you anything before I go?"

Jaybo looked away and waved his hand. "No, thanks. The ladies will take care of me."

*****

After filling his gas tank and doing a few errands, Lang had a late lunch at Gracie's. Relieved not to run into anyone he knew, he paid Stacy and headed out. "Tell Gracie I'll miss her sandwiches," he said, tipping his hat at the redhead, who was clearly smitten.

"Oh, you're leavin' us?" Stacy looked stricken and wrung her hands on a very dirty apron.

"Yup, gotta get back home. Work's waitin."

"Bet your folks are sorry to see you go. How's your dad? I heard he was in the hospital."

"Home now, recovering with lots of people fussing over him. Should make a full recovery."

"That's great. Well, see ya."

He tipped his hat again and stepped back into the afternoon heat.

CHAPTER 45

As Lang headed through the Morgan's Run gates, he thought about what he wanted to say to Beth. What could he say? What was there to say? It was after three, and he hoped she would still be at the farm. He didn't think he could face a whole contingent of Morgans at the big house. As he headed up the rise to the farm road, Maggie's truck passed by. She waved and gave him a thumbs-up.

When Lang pulled up beside the farm office, Ruthie and Raoul were perched on a fence rail, chatting. "Hey, Lang!" she called, hopping down as Raoul turned and headed toward the processing barns.

"Hey, Ruthie. How're you doin'?"

"Great. I hear you're leavin' us soon?"

"Tomorrow morning bright and early, I'm 'fraid. Is Beth around?"

Ruthie paused, unsure of what she should say. She knew her sister had been ignoring Lang's calls. Should she risk her sister's wrath and tell him where to find her? "I'm not sure she wants to see you, buddy."

"I know she doesn't, but please, Ruthie. Give me a break. I only want five minutes to say goodbye. Then I'll be out of her hair and everyone else's."

"I'll probably regret this tonight, but she's down in the west beds or maybe with the lambs, a little further out. Behind the barns—just follow the path, or ask one of the guys when you get out there."

"Thanks, Ruthie."

"If I'm not here when you get back, good luck. Sorry you couldn't stay around longer. You're missin' a great fair this weekend."

"So I hear. Take care, Ruthie." He gave her a hug. "Maybe by the next time I'm back in Saguaro, you'll be hitched to a certain cowboy."

She laughed. "Yeah, right. And, our pigs'll be flying round the Valley, too."

*****

The afternoon sun still scorching, he walked between fields of corn on one side and all manner of vegetables, fruits, and flowers on the other. The farm gardens stretched for miles in all directions. He was again awestruck at the vastness of their operation. After asking several farm hands along the way, he finally spotted Beth in one of the open meadows, brush in hand, beside a lamb whose mother stood nearby, watching. Even from a distance, he marveled at her gentleness as she brushed the tiny creature, its head resting on her shoulder.

Afraid of startling her, he called as he approached, and she turned. She nodded, but kept her place on the ground, continuing to stroke and brush the lamb. With Lang's appearance, the day's calm was shattered. She leaned against the creature, deriving small comfort from its warmth as she struggled to collect herself. "Getting her ready for Saturday," she said softly, gazing up to meet his eyes.

"She's a beauty." *As are you*, he thought, watching the curve of her strong arm as she cradled the lamb against her chest. It seemed almost a dream now, their lovemaking, as if his head had never rested against that same chest, and his lips had never traced every inch of her. His own chest ached with emptiness and longing.

"Yes, she is. Course, I'll have to do this all over again Saturday morning. Soon as I'm through, she'll go roll in mud or worse." She turned back to the lamb, unable to look at Lang. The man she had loved so wantonly, so intensely. Of course, he looked gorgeous as usual, a slight tear on the sleeve of his faded Rambler Sports tee shirt revealed the strong shoulder she had kissed, bitten, and stroked with a passion she didn't know she possessed.

"Beth, I'm sorry."

Reluctantly, she stopped brushing and gave the lamb a pat on her rump. She scampered off to join her mother. "For what?"

"For taking advantage of you at a vulnerable time."

She stood and grabbed her backpack, then walked toward him. "We've been through this before, Lang. You didn't do anything that needs an apology. I was a willing participant in all of it."

"Yes, but—"

She raised one hand. "No buts, please. You're leaving. Let's just say goodbye and get on with things."

"Is that what you want?"

She shrugged, eyes full of sadness as she gazed out across the fields. "I believe we've already established that at this moment in my history, I am incapable of knowing what I want."

Lang surprised himself by saying, "You could come to Boston?" He did not want to let her go. Suddenly going back to his well-ordered life, stepping back into his apartment and work, seemed empty without her.

"For what?"

"To get away, clear your head, figure things out."

"Not a good idea."

"Why?"

"Because I'm a basket case."

"That's why it's a good idea. Get some distance from all this."

"I can't. I may be a basket case, but I'm a basket case who's in love with you."

"Oh, Beth," he said, reaching for her as one of the trucks approached, several guys riding on the tailgate.

She stood back, gesturing to the driver to stop as she put herself out of Lang's reach.

"Please don't. I don't need your pity, and I don't expect you to say anything. I know you aren't in love with me, and I really don't want to hear any more."

The truck halted a short distance away, waiting for her. Beth's eyes softened as they met his. "I've got to go. I hope you have a safe trip."

"Beth, please, there's so much more to say."

"Not for me," she said softly. "Do you want a ride back?"

"No, thanks. I'll walk."

"Goodbye, Lang. Take care." She gave him a brief hug but refused to let him draw her closer. Then, without another word, Beth hopped up on the tailgate, and the truck disappeared in a cloud of dust.

When Lang reached the Rover, her truck was gone. *That's it, then. Why do I feel lonelier than I've ever been in my life?*

CHAPTER 46

"Nora, I don't know about this trip," Ben Senior said as husband and wife changed for dinner. The elder Morgans dressed for dinner, a ritual they had observed their entire lives, no matter how informal the occasion.

Exasperated, Leonora waved her hairbrush at him. "Everything will be fine."

"I'm worried about Bethie. Maybe we should take her with us?"

"On our second honeymoon? Don't be ridiculous. She wouldn't want to come, and she would be very angry if we put off the trip for her sake. She hates us hovering, as you well know."

"You know the last time I'd seen her cry before last week?"

"I know, I know, but maybe crying is good for her. Beth has always held everything inside, not like her crazy brothers and Ruthie. It's good for her to let it out."

"Don't get me wrong, sweetheart," he said, taking her in his arms. "There's nothing I want more than to spend time with the love of my life." He bent and kissed her forehead, then her lips.

Leonora kissed him, then pulled back. "Oh, no, you don't, you old charmer. I adore you, but you're not changing my mind with sweet talk."

He shrugged. "Can't blame a guy for tryin'. Anything for a kiss, darlin'."

"Come on, Romeo, I hear Emma callin' for us."

*****

The talk during dinner revolved around the fair and everyone's various activities. For the first time in their adult lives, the senior Morgans were attending as spectators, nothing more. Ben was manning the hospitality table, where brochures about the Lodge, spa, and pack trips would be displayed. Harley would be with the two horses they were showing, a Thoroughbred, Caspar, and Ben Senior's morgan, Royal. These horses were highly sought after for sire. Caspar was old and was seldom rode, but extremely valuable, a beautiful animal, one of the finest in the Valley.

Maggie, Jeb, and Emma were giving pony rides at the edge of the midway, and Morgan's Run would have the largest, most abundant farm stand at the fair, selling fresh produce, herbs, goat cheese, and an wide assortment salsas, jams, jellies, and pickles, made by Carmela and a group of women from the village who came to the big house once a month for canning day.

Beth, Ruthie, and Raoul would be with the farm's livestock. They were showing pigs, lambs, chickens, and a few prize goats.

As Carmela served the main course, an assortment of enchiladas, salads, and cold vegetables, Ben Senior gazed at his eldest daughter, who had not uttered a word during the family's lively discussion. "What time you taking the animals, Bethie?"

She looked up at him with sad eyes, her movements listless. "They told us we can set up anytime after three tomorrow afternoon."

Her father's heart ached for her, wishing he could take away her pain. Was this about that idiot Sampson, or had the Dillon boy's leaving put his precious child in such a state? He wanted to ask, but knew she would not—and perhaps could not—give him an answer. "Who's staying with 'em?"

"Raoul's got two kids. They're all excited. Already got their sleeping bags loaded in the trucks."

Unlike some ranch owners, the Morgans always made sure a hand or two stayed overnight at the fairgrounds with the livestock. Harley and Ben would transport the horses early Saturday morning, but the other animals were required to be there the day before. The judging would take place in the morning, and then all but the winners would be trucked home Saturday night.

Emma sighed. "I wish I could camp out with 'em."

"You need your beauty sleep, Sweet Pea," her father said, ruffling her curls. "Got to be sharp for those ponies."

She smiled proudly, beaming at Ben.

Gazing at his precious daughter, Ben Morgan's eyes filled, and he thought about how much his life had changed since she and her beautiful mother had come into it. Maggie saw his expression and smiled, then turned to look up at the cook. "Carmela, you've outdone yourself again. These are the best quesadillas I've ever had."

Beth watched her brother and sister-in-law and thought that Maggie had never looked more beautiful. Pregnancy and happiness certainly agreed with her.

She was interrupted in her reverie by Ruthie.

"Hey, sis, I thought with all the guys there with the livestock, I might head over and help Harley with Caspar and Royal. You know how much attention they get, and Harley isn't always great with the public."

"Your choice," Beth said, knowing full well the reason for her sister's defection. Without preamble, she pushed back from the table and stood up, nodding to her family one by one. "Would you excuse me, Mother? I'm really tired, and I think I'll head upstairs."

"Oh, my goodness, darlin', shall I come with you?"

"Absolutely not. Just tired. Gonna call it a day. See everyone tomorrow."

When they heard Beth's bedroom door shut, her brother shook his head and said, "If I could kill Bill Sampson and get away with it, I would, and Lang Dillon right behind him."

"Ben!" Maggie cried, spying the shock on her daughter's face.

"Just kiddin', Sweet Pea. Daddy's just sad for Aunt Beth."

"Me, too," Emma said, jutting her chin out.

With a warning look at her son, Leonora patted her granddaughter's head. "Let's hope the fair cheers her up, darlin'. Gonna be lots of fun."

CHAPTER 47

"S'posed to be a glorious weekend, thank goodness," Martha Dillon said, sneaking a glance at her husband, who was propped up in a chair next to her. He looked very uncomfortable but had insisted upon coming to the dinner table for Lang's last night. "There's nothing worse then trying to sell wine in a damp booth with cheese sweating and crackers soggy enough to sip."

"What time should we get there Saturday?" Rose asked.

"Well, Jon's going over with the men at dawn. Silly, really, because who wants to drink wine before noon? The men'll bring the coolers of white and probably a dozen cases of the reds. You and I can bring the cheeses, platters, and crackers over around nine. No sense in going earlier, as we won't open up until ten."

"Sure you wouldn't like to reconsider staying till Monday?" Rose said, winking at Lang.

Lang smiled at her, not daring to glance at his father. He had asked his mother repeatedly if she needed him, and she had almost ordered him to take off.

"Now I wish I hadn't shooed you away," his mother said. "Two gorgeous men and your beautiful sister and the wine'd be sailin' out of the crates. I could hide in the back and not scare anyone off."

"You're always the most beautiful gal at the fair," Jaybo said, reaching over to squeeze her hand. "Now, Ms. Partridge, if you and my son can help me up, I'm ready to head back to bed."

They both helped him up. Then Judy Partridge took over. "We're all set from here. Enjoy your dinner." As they headed down the hall to the study, they heard Jaybo say, "Bathroom, Partridge" before the study door closed behind them.

"Thank goodness we put that full bath in off the study two years ago," Martha whispered, setting down her fork and sipping a crisp white chardonnay. "Chicken was fabulous, Jon," she said, waving her plate away as Neecy and the cook began to clear. She turned to Lang. "What time will you be leaving in the morning, darlin'?"

"I'm gonna try for five. I have two appointments in Santa Fe for late afternoon."

"What about breakfast? Neecy? Jon?"

"Absolutely not," Lang said, raising a hand. "I'll get coffee on my way out of town."

"How about if I pack you a lunch?" Jon said, one hand on his hip, the other holding a stack of pottery. "I made up a big batch of chicken salad for us tomorrow."

"Thanks. That would be great."

"I'll pack it in one of the thermal winery takeout sacks and put it in the front of the main fridge, in case I'm not up when you head out."

"That sounds terrific, Jon."

Martha stood. "Well, kiddos, I better check on your dad. Lang, sweetheart, please come and say goodnight before you go up." She hugged him round the shoulders and patted Rose's arm.

"How about a nightcap on the porch?" Rose asked. Her brother had been unusually quiet all through dinner, and she was already missing him. Having him here, even briefly, had taken some of the worry over her parents off her shoulders.

"Seltzer water for me, sis."

"That sounds perfect. Neecy, have we got seltzer?"

Neecy smiled, setting down a tray. "You guys go on out. I'll bring it."

*****

Stars blanketed the sky. As they sat, several shooting stars blazed by. "I'll miss this," he said, setting his glass on the table and leaning back, hands behind his head. "It's pretty rare that we see more than a few stars in Boston."

"Then you'll have to come back soon."

"Maybe. Rosie, I already feel like such a shit for leaving you to deal with Dad."

"Don't. We've got lots of help. The main thing is to find someone to run the winery."

"What about Manual and the crew?"

"I'm talking about what Dad does. The PR, the schmoozing, the oversight. They've actually needed a full-time manager for a couple of years, but now they're gonna have to get serious."

"What'dya think? Will it be difficult?"

"Maybe not. Jon has lots of contacts in Napa, and he thinks he even knows a couple of people who might be interested."

"That's great."

"Can't come soon enough. I'm so far behind at work."

"Oh, Rosie, I'm sorry."

"Don't be. I could have stayed on the east coast and gone with Dr. Heavers to Baltimore. I chose to come back."

"Do you regret it?"

"No. The Valley's my home. This is my community, for better or worse."

"Seems like that's what Beth thinks, too."

"How did it go? Your talk with her?"

"Pretty much goodbye and good luck."

"Do you love her?"

"Yes." There, he had finally admitted it. "I love her more than I've ever loved any woman, except you, dear sister."

Mouth agape, Rose stared at him. She was well aware of her brother's feelings for Beth Morgan, but shocked that he had finally owned up to them. "Did you tell her?"

"What's the point?"

"What do you mean, what's the point? You love her and she loves you. You belong together."

"You forget, Dear Abby, that my home is three thousand miles away, and her home is here."

"You'll figure it out."

"Besides, after her breakup with Bill, she doesn't know what she feels right now. For all I know, their cozy lunch at La Forge was the start of their reconciliation."

"That's bullshit and you know it, Lang Dillon!"

Now it was his turn to stare open-mouthed at his usually prim and proper sister.

"Don't give me that look," she said, rolling her eyes. "I can swear when it suits me. And how, pray tell, do you imagine Beth and Bill can reconcile when she's crazy, head-over-heels in love with you?"

"She doesn't know what she feels. That's my point."

"I beg to differ. I've known Beth Morgan my entire life, and I've never seen her look at anyone the way she looks at you. She's never been gaga over anyone. Yes, she loved Bill, but it was not the kind of love that she feels for you. You've lit quite a flame under the quiet Morgan sister. She's never going to be the same."

Suddenly weary, he reached over and drained his glass. "It's over, Rosie. Maybe when I get home and sort things out, I'll realize this visit has been a dream and I'll wake up and be me again."

"Cilla will be waiting!"

"Not gonna happen. We live on different planets now. Besides, she texted to say Brent met her at Logan with an engagement ring."

"Well, that's one piece of good news. You going in to say 'bye to Mom and Dad?"

Rose followed him as he knocked on the study door. His father was half asleep, heavily sedated. Judy Partridge appeared to be tidying up, and their mother was nowhere to be seen. Lang bent over the bed and took his father's hand. "Hey, Dad, I've just come to say goodbye."

His father grunted, and his eyes fluttered open and shut. "Safe trip, son," he mumbled. Lang kissed his forehead, then stepped back, wondering if this would be the last time he saw his father alive.

He found his mother in the kitchen, helping Jon and Neecy pack cheeses and bags of crackers. She gazed at him sadly. "You going up, darlin'?"

"Yup."

"We're gonna miss you something terrible, aren't we?" she said to the other three.

"Sure are," Neecy said.

"I'll be back, Mom, I promise. If things get worse, I can fly out. I can also fly out to help with the new hiring. That's one thing I'm good at."

"Thank you, dearie. We'll give a shout if we need you."

They hugged, and when Lang stepped back, he saw tears in her eyes. Gazing around the room, he found Rose and Neecy misty-eyed, Jon busying himself with cleaning up to hide his emotions.

"I'll try to get up to see you off," Martha said. "But I'm not a good early riser anymore."

"Please sleep in, Mom. You've gotta rest for the weekend."

After more hugs and kisses, the party separated. Rose and Lang went upstairs, and the others continued their work.

At Rose's door, Lang turned and gazed down at his beloved sibling. "It's been great to spend time with you, Rosie. Will you come to Boston soon?"

"Maybe when things settle down here. I'd like to head east at some point to see Dr. Heavers."

They hugged, and as Rose pulled away, she met his eyes. "Tell her, please, Lang. If you don't, you'll regret it for the rest of your life."

"Someday, Rosie."

Someday will be too late, Rose thought, stepping into her room and closing the door.

CHAPTER 48

Beth woke shortly after sunrise Friday morning with a dull ache in the pit of her stomach and a sadness that touched every part of her body. After she showered and dressed, the ache had subsided a little, but she could not shake the sadness. Finally, at six-fifteen, she jumped in the truck and headed for the Dillons'. She wasn't sure why she was going and had not the slightest idea what she would say to Lang, but she needed to see him one last time.

Stillness enveloped her as she stepped from the truck, feeling foolish and intrusive. Lang's Rover wasn't there, but that wasn't unusual, as he often parked at the winery. She was about to back up when she spied a lone figure on the porch, Rose in bathrobe and slippers. She waved and came down the steps.

"He's gone, Beth. Left about five, I think. I missed him, too."

"Oh, of course. He'd want to beat the heat."

Rose regarded her, hazel eyes thoughtful. "There's always his cell, you know. And Boston's a great place to visit."

Beth sat hard on the steps, head in hands. "Oh, Rose, what you must think of me. What a ninny I've been."

Rose sat beside her and patted her knee. "I don't think you're a ninny. If anyone's the ninny, it's my brother." *Who loves you,* she refrained from adding. Much as she wanted to ease Beth's distress, they were Lang's words to say, when he was ready.

"No, he isn't. He's a kind man who befriended me at a time when I desperately needed a friend. And then, what did I do? I backed him into a corner, expecting declarations of love and who knows what else, when I didn't have the slightest idea what I was doing."

"Give it time. *Patience* might be the operative word in this situation. Lang cares about you. He'll be in touch, and I'm sure he'd love to hear from you."

Beth turned to her and smiled. Rose's usually carefully combed hair was askew, ruffled with sleep. "Thanks, Rose. You working at the fair?"

"Oh, yes. Mother, Jon, and I are working the winery table. You?"

"Ruthie and I'll be with the animals. My brothers come tonight. I'll send Sam over to buy a few bottles of my favorite wines in case I don't get out of the pens. Ruthie's a big fan of the rides and likes to take lots of breaks."

"Hope to see you there, but Beth, you know very well no Morgan needs to buy wine from a Dillon."

"Yes, but Sam doesn't know that," Beth said, a twinkle in her eye as she rose and said her goodbyes.

*****

Already eighty miles from the Valley, Lang wondered if he would ever fill the loneliness he felt driving out of the Valley. This was the place he had spent his whole life escaping, and now its loss gnawed at him. He could not even distract himself with work since every other canyon found him in a dead zone and his cell phone service cut out.

His revelation to Rosie had floored him. He wasn't quite sure what to do with the realization that he loved Beth. He could not imagine living three thousand miles away from her for a day, week, or month, never mind the years that stretched ahead. He missed her beautiful eyes, gazing at him without a hint of guile. She had trusting, gentle eyes. The feel of her skin on his, her slender body, soft in places that fit him perfectly. Had it all been physical? *Our emotional and intellectual fit are there. What would happen if we took a lifetime to explore the rest?*

Finally, Lang decided that the best course would be to go home, settle in to familiar routines, and then plan his next move. Beth had spent much of their time together telling *him* what a basket case *she* was, but truth be told, the trip back to the Valley had thrown him for a loop in more ways than one. He didn't want to hate his father, for example, but his feelings were so wrapped up in less than happy childhood memories and the fierce protectiveness he felt for his mother. *What protectiveness?* he asked himself. *What the hell can I do from three thousand miles away? I've been perfectly happy to let Mother fend for herself and let Rosie take care of things. What a first class shit you are, Lang Dillon,* he thought as he crossed the border into New Mexico. *Time to prepare for the clients,* he decided, and he put his pathetic life aside for a few hours, at least.

CHAPTER 49

Kyle had been watching his older sister all evening. He had never seen her look so defeated and sad. "So, what's the plan?" he asked, gazing around the dinner table as he served himself a spoonful of Carmela's tender greens. They were eating early so all would be rested for the fair and Emma, especially, could get a good night's sleep. They ate on the terrace. The night was warm with clear skies. Carmela had prepared a savory polenta, several huge salads, and a variety of steamed greens and vegetables. She also served a platter of tacos, some stuffed with slices of portabella mushrooms and others with farm-raised beef, lettuces, and local cheeses, with her salsas on the side.

"We can always use help at the farm stand," Ruthie said.

"So you can float freely?" Ben asked, helping himself to portabella tacos and serving Emma one from the beef platter.

"Ha, ha," Ruthie said, glaring at her brother.

They all knew that given her druthers, Ruthie would find her way to the horse paddocks, ostensibly to check on whether a certain gorgeous wrangler needed assistance. Harley grinned but said nothing.

"Well, I'm helping Ms. Emma and Maggie with the pony rides," Robbie said, winking at his niece. Emma adored all of her aunts and uncles, but she worshipped Uncle Robbie.

Emma clapped and Maggie said, "That'll be terrific. We need all the help we can get."

"I'll join Raoul and the crew at the stand," Sam said.

Beth smiled at him, recalling her early morning conversation with Rose. The farm stand was only a few short steps from the Saguaro Valley Winery table. How convenient. "They'll appreciate it. Thanks, Sam."

"I see no one's offered to help me at the meet and greet?" Ben said, pretending to look hurt.

"Well, I can stop by," his father said.

Leonora glared at her oldest son. "Dad and I will stroll by, and that's all. This is our year to enjoy the fair, remember?"

"But if—"

"No buts, Dad," Ben said. "I've got it covered. Mel and Jim'll be with me, too." Even though they had only recently promoted Jim Thompson to official manager, he had been with the ranch for fifteen years and had capably overseen the day-to-day running of the Lodge and staff. Mel Farrell and her life partner, Rita Lazares, ran the spa. Mel had been with them nine years, and the Lodge and spa's business had tripled under her auspices. If anyone could sell the tourists on the ranch, it was Mel.

"No Rita?" Leonora asked, frowning.

Ben shook his head, grinning at Harley. "Not with the group that just arrived. They want yoga classes around the clock. She's booked for regular classes and a bunch of private sessions all weekend."

"What about the fair?" Ruthie said.

"Apparently some of the group are not into the fair scene," her brother said, heaping a second helping of greens onto his plate.

Their father whistled. "Whoa, Nelly, you boys're gonna have yer hands full next week, Harley."

"Don't go there," Harley said, sipping a beer.

Staring at Harley in disbelief, Ruthie, who could not imagine anyone at any age not wanting to spent the weekend at the Valley Fair, she said, "What about the kids? Don't they want to go?"

"Nannies," Ben said.

"Nannies?" Beth repeated, staring at her brother. "Are nannies going on the pack trip?"

"Oh, yes," Harley said. "Three of 'em. Two have never been on a horse before."

Everyone burst out laughing, Kyle and Robbie the loudest. Finally, Robbie said, "What the hell are you going to do?"

"Pray," Ben said, eyeing his brother with a shake of his head.

"Let's change the subject, shall we?" Leonora said, waving for Carmela to begin clearing. "Anyone need a ride with Dad and me tomorrow?"

*****

Maggie, Ben, and Emma said their goodbyes right after dessert, and the rest of the family began to disperse for last minute preparations and bed. As Beth headed up, Kyle caught her in the hall. "How're you doin', sis?"

"Okay."

"Didn't look okay at dinner."

"I'll get there."

"Sign me up with the lambs and pigs. What time are you headed out?"

"Six."

"Can I hitch a ride?"

"Of course. Thanks, Kyle."

"He's an idiot."

"Don't start on poor Bill again. It's all settled. We're moving on, selling the condo. He's sorry and that's that."

Kyle placed a hand on her shoulder and leaned forward to kiss her cheek. "I wasn't talking about Bill Sampson, but he's an idiot, too. Night, Bethie."

*****

"This was an incredible meal, thanks," Lang told his clients, Rachel and Dave Ferris.

"Our pleasure. Was great to finally meet the brains behind Rambler Sports," Dave said, shaking his hand. Ferris owned a chain of upscale clothing stores in the southwest, most in or around Santa Fe. They stocked many of the company's line, and Dave himself, a blond, tanned, ruggedly handsome fortysomething cowboy, and his slender, blonde, doe-eyed wife were perfect models for Rambler Sports clothing.

Lang laughed. "One of the brains, and certainly not the most creative one."

"I wish you'd stay with us tonight," Rachel said. "We have plenty of room. Much quieter than the Oleander."

"Thanks, but I'm all checked in. I'll sleep like a log and be on the road by five."

"Are you okay?" she asked, the question coming out of the blue. Dave stared at his wife, startled at her query.

Lang met her eyes and said quietly, "No, but I'll get there. I kind of left my heart in the Valley."

"Oh, that's sad," she said as the two men walked toward the Rover, leaving her silhouetted in the light of the arched doorway.

"Sorry, Lang," Dave said. "Rachel can be a bit of a mother hen at times."

"No problem. I probably look like a lost soul right now, and she picked up on it."

"Not our business."

"No, sadly, it's mine," Lang said, shaking Dave's hand. "Thanks for everything."

CHAPTER 50

"Did you see her face last night, Nora?" the elder Morgans sat alone at breakfast, their offspring long gone to the Fair. "I don't know if our Bethie's ever gonna get through this."

"She will be just fine, darlin', and don't think I don't know this is more hemming and hawing about the trip."

"I want to go, sweetheart, especially to be with you. I just wish it wasn't so long, that's all."

"Two months will fly by."

Her husband nodded, and Leonora knew just what he was thinking. It wasn't the kids or worry about Beth. It was two months away from his beloved home. Getting Ben Morgan to the theater in Phoenix or Tucson was like pulling teeth.

The prospect of being dragged round the world was practically killing him. Ever since the doctor's diagnosis, they knew they were living on borrowed time. She wanted to use that precious time together to travel, but he wanted to be home.

"Listen, I'll make you a deal. Let's try it, and if you're really homesick, we'll head home after the first cruise. That way I'll get to see most of Europe, and we can save the Mediterranean for the next time. It might've been a bit much to book two trips back to back."

He patted her hand. "Once we're in the saddle, I'll probably be fine, honey."

Leonora leaned over and kissed him. "Sure you will, darlin'. Now we'd better get a move on. The fair'll be over 'fore we get there."

*****

Lang woke at dawn, out of sorts after a restless night. He showered and dressed quickly, grabbing coffee and a bagel in the lobby before checking out. The Oleander was a lovely old inn, dreamy and romantic, tucked away in a quiet corner of the city. He noticed none of it until he started for the parking lot and passed an open courtyard. Through the archway he spied a lush garden area, surrounded on all sides by walls festooned with flowering vines, hanging pots, and brightly colored tile work. Lang stopped and stood, gazing inward, sipping his coffee, transported back to the Red Mesa Inn and the magical evening he had spent with Beth.

"Beautiful, isn't it?" The man's voice startled him and he jumped. "So sorry, sir. I'm Ned Taylor, one of the owners here. You coming or going?"

"Going, I'm 'fraid. Didn't notice this last night."

"No, it was booked for a small wedding party. *Southwest Quarterly* just dubbed it the most romantic restaurant spot in the southwest."

They must not have visited the Red Mesa, Lang thought, nodding. "It's a pretty spot. Reminds me of another place."

"Red Mesa's secret garden, I'll wager."

"You know it?"

"Chip Redrock is my brother-in-law. When my wife Charlene and I remodeled here, we visited her brother and took lots of pictures and measurements."

"Small world."

"Yes, it is. You'll have to come back to see us again and bring the woman you were just thinking about."

"I beg your pardon?"

Ned Taylor smiled. "Would you excuse me? Duty calls. Have a safe trip wherever you're headed. Good day."

*****

The Valley Fair stretched for acres and acres to the north of the village. Some of the land was the Morgan's ranch grazing pasture, some owned by other ranchers and some federal and state park. Once a year, the land was mowed and groomed. Fences were removed and repositioned to make way for the midway, stalls for livestock, and over two acres of booths, tables, and open markets selling everything from high-end silver jewelry to homemade fudge. All the local ranches had tables or booths, and most of the village shops as well. Gabriella passed Beth and waved as she carried armloads of clothing to her prime spot just off the midway.

"Who's that?" Kyle asked. "That's not that wacky ladies dress shop owner from town, is it?"

Beth laughed and shushed him. "The very one. She actually has really nice things. Both mom and I have been shopping there recently."

"I wouldn't spread that around if I were you."

"Ha, ha. Now let's get the brushes out. These lambs looks as though they've been through a war."

Ruthie had already disappeared. As soon as they unloaded, she'd told them she would grab coffees and muffins and be right back, and that had been an hour earlier.

"I'm starving," Kyle said. "What'dya think? Should we wait for our lovesick sister to return, or should I go get us something?"

Beth laughed, throwing him a brush. "Call her cell, why don't you? I don't want to end up here alone if the judges come by."

A few minutes later, the errant Ruthie appeared, laden with bags of muffins and sausage rolls and a tray with three large coffees. "Sorry it took so long. The line was unbelievable."

"Especially when you take a detour around the horse stalls, Kyle said."

"Very funny! Do you want your coffee or not?"

"Did you see Emma?" Beth asked, taking a muffin from the bag.

"Yup. She's about to burst a button, she's so excited. They have a long line waiting for rides."

The bustle of the fair swallowed them up. They were surrounded by every kind of fresh local food you could want as well as a Ferris wheel, pony rides, and midway games. The bustle of the day carried Beth away, and for a few hours, she put aside the grief and sadness to enjoy the exuberant embrace of the close-knit

Valley community. People traveled from hundreds of miles to the fair, but it was the locals who carried the weekend, the crowning glory of yet another year of hard work.

Midmorning, she got a text from Bill saying he missed being there, and he wished her a fun day. She deleted it, shoving memories of previous fairs they had enjoyed from her mind. Then she turned off her phone and threw it into her backpack just as the judges arrived to look over their animals, now groomed and festooned with ribbons.

CHAPTER 51

Late afternoon, Kyle and Beth fed the livestock and turned their care over to the three teenagers Raoul had hired to spend the night with them. Two of the lambs had won prizes, as had one of their Red Wattle pigs. Most of the chickens and roosters had been sold, and the rest of the lambs as well. They would take the lambs back to the ranch and Enos Walker would slaughter and deliver them.

Arm and arm, brother and sister headed for the bustling midway. "What'dya say, sis?" Kyle said. "Fancy a ride on the Ferris wheel?"

"I dunno. Why don't you go and I'll observe?"

"Nothin' doin'. Look, Emma, Ben, and Maggie are getting on. Come on! I bought a bunch of tickets earlier for just this eventuality."

Kyle pulled her toward the line. It appeared that, like it or not, there would be room on the next turn for them. As they reached the gate, Beth was in front of him, marching stoically toward the open swing. She did not see the hand on her brother's shoulder or see him step aside to give away his place. She was already seated in one of the last cars on that turn when Lang slipped in beside her.

"Don't scream, please. It will scare the kids." Warm eyes gazed into hers. Lang took her hand as the operator locked their crossbar into place and the Ferris wheel began its turn. "Besides, screaming will spoil what I want to say."

"Lang, what in the world? Why are you here? You should be halfway across Texas by now." She paused, staring hard at his sky-blue eyes as they turned gray in the light of late afternoon. "I must look like a fright, covered in dirt and sawdust and smelling like the barnyard."

"You've never looked more beautiful, my darling."

"What did you want to say?"

Lang took both her hands in his and forced himself to block out the looks of every Morgan and a number of other Valley people, including his mother and sister, on the ground and on the turning wheel. "I love you, Beth, more than anything else in the world. I cannot go anywhere if you're not there. I want to spend the rest of my life with you, and I refuse to waste another minute. Marry me? Please, my darling, please say yes and make me the happiest man on earth."

"Oh, Lang, I love you so much. I can't believe you came back."

"Is that a yes?"

"Yes," she said softly, her arms circling his neck.

Lang's lips found hers as their swing neared the ground and started another upward swing. Hoots, hollers, whistles, and clapping accompanied their ascent. "I think we have a bit of an audience," he said huskily, eyes gazing down at her with love.

"It's the Valley, darlin'. You might as well get used to it, unless you're planning on a bicoastal marriage?"

"Never. This is where you belong, so I do, too."

EPILOGUE

Beth and Lang decided to marry on her birthday, August first which gave them a year to plan and begin work, set on a lovely hillside about a mile from Maggie and Ben, at the northwest corner of Dillon land. Sam Morgan was working with them and had designed a beautiful modern home that blended with its surroundings as if it had been there forever.

Finally, it was time for Leonora and Ben Senior to head off on their two months of back-to-back cruises. Lang flew back to Boston to pack up his condo. At least for now, he planned to keep it as an investment as it was in a prime spot in Cambridge and had already tripled in value since he purchased it. After much discussion, some of which featured Lang falling on his sword and offering to step away from the company, his partners had proposed he stay on and that they establish Rambler Sports West, with all their usual lines as well as the one-of-a-kind riding gear they were developing for disabled riders. This would allow him time to help manage the winery until they found the right person to take over.

He had been away less than a week but spoke to Beth three and four times a day, more if he could locate her. Toward the end of his stay, condo packed up, he phoned late one evening from his hotel room at the Marlowe. "Hey, sweetheart. I'm missing you so much it hurts."

"You in your room?"

"Yup. Where'd you think I'd be at eleven at night?"

"Just wondering."

"Your voice sounds funny. Beth, is everything alright?"

"Absolutely. Never better."

"You haven't found anyone else, have you?"

"No, and I hope you haven't. Otherwise the next few minutes might be a little embarrassing."

"Beth, you're starting to scare me. What's going on?" Someone knocked at the door, and Lang hopped up. "Who the heck's that? Hold on, sweetheart."

When Lang opened the door, he found her, ear to her phone, small bag slung over her shoulder. "Got room for one more in there?" she asked, smiling.

As his arms reached out, drawing her close, Lang experienced what was now becoming a familiar sensation. In Beth Morgan's arms, he was home. For the first time in his life.

"I love you," she whispered, trailing kisses down his neck.

"I love you, too, my beautiful cowgirl. Come in and let me show you how much."

Please read on to preview chapters from ***Jeb's Promise: Book Three in the Morgan's Run Romances***

About the Author

M. Lee Prescott is the author of dozens of works of fiction for adults, young adults, and children, among them **Prepped to Kill, Gadfly, Lost in Spindle City (Ricky Steele Mysteries), A Friend of Silence, In the Name of Silence and The Silence of Memory (Roger and Bess Mysteries) Jigsaw, Song of the Spirit**, and her newest contemporary romance series, **Morgan's Run,** of which **Lang's Return** is the second! Three of her nonfiction titles have been published by Heinemann, and she has published numerous articles in the field of literacy education. Lee is a professor of education at a small New England liberal arts college, where she teaches reading and writing pedagogy. Her current research focuses on mindfulness and connections to reading and writing. She regularly teaches abroad, most recently in Singapore.

Lee has lived in southern California (loved those Laguna nights!), Chapel Hill, North Carolina, and various spots in Massachusetts and Rhode Island. Currently she resides in Massachusetts on a beautiful river, where she canoes, swims, and watches an incredible variety of wildlife pass by. She is the mother of two grown sons and spends lots of time with them, their beautiful wives, and her amazing grandchildren. When not teaching or writing, Lee's passions revolve around family, yoga (Kripalu is a second home), swimming, sharing mindfulness with children and adults, and walking.

Lee loves to hear from readers. Email her anytime at <u>mleeprescott@gmail.com</u>, and visit her website to hear the latest and sign up for her newsletters!

<u>AUTHOR WEBPAGE AND NEWSLETTER SIGN UP</u>

A Note from the Author

I am thrilled to bring you Beth and Lang's story, the second of what I hope will be *many* **Morgan's Run** books. Thank you so much for reading. Just as Maggie and Ben do, Beth and Lang will stay, changing and growing as this series progresses. The Morgan's Run books are set in the gorgeous American southwest, an area of the country that is dear to my heart because it is home to my youngest son and family, but also because its beauty is so extraordinary and so startlingly different from that of my New England home. What a backdrop for romance and adventure!

If you liked ***Lang's Return*** and would be willing to write an Amazon review, I would very much appreciate it! In fact, I will be happy to send my first two reviewers a free copy **of another of my titles!** If you submit a review, just email me at mleeprescott@gmail.com with your name and address and I will see that you receive your free copy of whichever title you choose!

If you would like to sign up for future book releases and occasional notices about my books, please visit my Author Website and sign up for my newsletter. I promise I will not share your address, nor will I flood you with emails. Do visit my site to read more about my books and to hear what's next. By the end of the year, I hope to have Ricky Steele's fourth adventure out, as well as more Morgan's Run stories and the third Roger and Bess Mystery, ***The Silence of Memory***. Time will tell if I'm successful!

Finally, this book has been revised, proofed, and edited many, many times, but my intrepid assistants and I are human, so if you spot a typo, please email me at mleeprescott@gmail.com and I will fix it. If you'd like to know more about my other books, please scroll ahead to the next section, which is followed by sample chapters of the third **Morgan's Run** book, *Jeb's Promise.*

Warm wishes,
M. Lee Prescott

Contemporary romances and mysteries by M. Lee Prescott include:

The Ricky Steele Mysteries
Book 1: Prepped to Kill
Book 2: Gadfly
Book 3: Lost in Spindle City

Also featuring Ricky Steele:
Jigsaw

Roger and Bess Mysteries
Book 1: A Friend of Silence
Book 2: In the Name of Silence
Book 3: The Silence of Memory

Contemporary Romances

Well Loved Romances
Widow's Island
Hestor's Way
Glass Walls (coming soon!)

Morgan's Run Romances
Book 1: Emma's Dream
Book 2: Lang's Return
Book 3: Jeb's Promise

Young Adult Historical Romance
Song of the Spirit

CHAPTER 1

"You can do this, cowboy."

Jeb spoke the words aloud as he pulled the jeep alongside the barn. An hour early for work, he wanted to get settled in on his first day back before the rest barreled in.

"Your parents were great, Jebo!"

"Yeah, right. They loved you, that's for sure. Who wouldn't? Now, if their good-for-nothing cowboy son could just go to college, everything would be hunky-dory."

"Let's have a picnic tomorrow. Who knows when we'll both get another day off at the same time?"

He reached down and felt the ring in his pocket, the beautiful engagement ring he had picked out a month earlier. Tomorrow I pop the question, *he thought, just as lights blinded him and a deafening boom descended.*

"Hello, are you in charge here?"

Lost in remembering, he hadn't heard the car approach. He turned to spy a young woman hopping out of a huge white SUV. About his age, she wore jeans, new shiny boots, and what looked like a brand new Morgan's Run tee shirt in the ranch's newest color, coral. If he hadn't been off the market, she was definitely his type. Petite, curvy, and fair-skinned, her shoulder-length auburn hair was held back in a loose ponytail. She held a ranch baseball cap in one hand, backpack in the other.

"Me, in charge? Not by a long shot. Can I help you?"

"I was told I could come down and go for a ride."

"Excuse me?"

"Ride. You know, on horseback?"

Ignoring her sarcasm, his eyes took in every inch of her. She might be stunning in her new cowgirl duds, but who the hell did she think she was? Boots looked like they'd just come out of the box, the jeans right behind them.

"Who gave you the idea that you could come down at sunrise and go for a ride? Are you staying on the ranch?"

She nodded. "And you are?"

"Jeb Barnes. I work here."

"Well, then, you must not have gotten the message."

"From?"

"Mr. Morgan. He called and talked to someone yesterday."

"So you're staying with the Morgans?"

"We're at the Lodge, for the wedding?"

The wedding! He'd been so wrapped up in grief and recovery that he'd totally forgotten about the eldest Morgan daughter Beth's wedding. It was sometime soon. The invitation was tacked to his fridge, but for the life of him, he couldn't remember the date.

"Oh, gee, I thought the wedding was a ways off."

"It is. Four weeks, actually. My dad dragged me here early for a vacation."

Jeb shook himself. "Sorry. I've been away so I'm kind of out of it."

On a different planet, more like it. Amy Foster stared at the young cowboy. A deep scar ran across his forehead, the wound fairly recent by the look of it. Other than that, he was perfect, if you liked cowboys, which she didn't. Her dad had dragged her along on this trip, and she couldn't wait to get through it and back to civilization. Still, the man standing in front of her was awfully cute. His reddish-brown hair curled under his Stetson. His tan face was sprinkled with freckles. He was about her height, five-eight, and broad-shouldered, all wiry muscle. When she met his eyes, she was surprised to see sadness reflected in their gray blue depths.

"I think we've gotten off to a bad start," she said, extending her hand. "I'm Amy Foster. My dad and Mr. Morgan were roommates in college. We just got in last night, and I asked if I might take a ride this morning."

"Jeb Barnes." He stepped forward and shook her hand, surprised to feel sparks as their hands connected. *Maybe you came back too soon, cowboy. Surely this ain't s'posed to be happening so soon after Stacy.*

He shook himself. "Are you an experienced rider?"

"Yes. Been riding since I was five. Mostly lessons in the ring or barn, though. Never ever been out on a trail. In fact, I was hoping someone around here might be bored enough to ride out with me."

Jeb grinned. "People rarely get bored around here."

Watch out, Amy Foster! You've sworn off men, and this guy has a smile that almost has you drooling.

As they stared at each other, a battered green truck pulled up and a tall, rugged cowboy stepped out. "Hey, buddy, welcome back!"

"Hey, Harley. Good to see you."

As Amy watched, the two men hugged and patted each other's backs. The newcomer was drop-dead gorgeous. What male around here wasn't? *He may be a poster cowboy with that sandy hair and killer smile, but my money's still on Jeb Barnes.*

After greeting his boss, Jeb remembered her and stepped aside. "Amy Foster, this is my boss, Harley Langdon. He runs the stables."

"Pleased to meet you, Ms. Foster." Harley came to shake her hand. "Mr. Morgan called about you last night."

"Yes. Would it be okay if I take a ride?"

"Not alone." He stepped back, scratched his head. "We've got a couple of lessons, but the kids can handle those. I've got…let's see. Hey, why doesn't Jeb take you?"

"But, boss, I just got back."

"A perfect way to ease back into things. You take Ms. Foster out for an hour or so. Then we can go over things. Maggie's bringing the baby by around ten to talk about the camp opening. Long as you're back by then, you've got plenty of time." He referred to Maggie Morgan, wife of the eldest Morgan son, Ben. Until the baby's birth six months earlier, Maggie, assisted by Jeb, had run most of the lessons and pony camps while Harley managed the stables and led pack trips for the ranch's wealthy clientele.

"But—"

"No buts about it. Go get Tara for Ms. Foster, and you take either Rowdy or Royal. We won't need 'em this morning."

Amy watched the interplay between the two handsome cowboys and wondered why Jeb Barnes had been away. Did it have something to do with that angry scar across his forehead and his sad eyes?

"Come on in, Ms. Foster."

"Amy, please," she said, trailing behind him. She doubted Barnes had heard her as he sprinted into the barn.

Chapter 2

"I was thinking we'd take an easy trail that winds around Echo Lake. Not too hilly and should take us about forty-five minutes."

"Sounds good," she called to his retreating back as her gentle sorrel morgan followed his. The rider and horse ahead of her moved as one, giving Amy a chance to study the man's strong, sturdy back, straining at his faded ranch tee shirt. The sun was already scorching hot. As they started off, he tied his flannel shirt round his waist.

Ordinarily, Jeb would have followed her, but she looked comfortable in the saddle, if a bit nervous, and he decided he should lead until they reached the high meadow. They rode at a leisurely pace, the horses comfortable on the familiar, meandering trail. As they reached open ground and the valley stretched out in front of them, he circled Royal round so they rode side by side. "You doin' okay?"

"Absolutely! It's beautiful up here, isn't it?"

"Prettiest valley in the world."

They gazed across the fields to the mountains running north and south, each silent for a few minutes. Finally she said, "It's so green. When Dad said we were coming to Saguaro Valley, I pictured dry desert. That looks like a huge tract of farmland." She pointed to the southwest.

"All Morgan's Run. Biggest organic farm in this part of the country."

"But how do they keep it green?"

"It's winter now, so most of Arizona is pretty green, but we're green all year here. Really unusual. At least for this part of the country. An orographic effect, creating unusual moisture laden cloud cover had created this green valley surrounded by desert on either side of the mountains to the east and west. Saguaro Canyon's the town, but everyone calls it Saguaro. The Valley's what they call 'undiscovered,' thanks to mega-wealthy ranchers like Ben Morgan and a handful of others."

"How'd they manage that?"

Jeb grinned and she blushed, averting her eyes. After the colossally self-absorbed Ryan had broken her heart, Amy had sworn off men, but this cute cowboy was already begging her to bend the rules.

"Mega bucks, as I said. They bought up all the land, created their huge ranches, and had their lawyers write up docs that ensured no one could subdivide the giant land parcels."

"That's gonna make my dad furious. Minute we got here he was talking vacation property."

"Good luck with that. If he's got money, he can probably get his college buddy to help him find something. As I say, Ben Morgan and a handful of his rancher friends own the Valley."

"Have you always lived here?"

"Since after high school. Was raised in Flagstaff, but then I got the job at Morgan's Run. Been here five years. The Morgans are good bosses. Really generous."

"Do you live on the ranch?"

His face drained of color, and he shook his head. "Started out in the bunkhouses, but then I moved."

"To?"

"Apartment in town. What'dya think? Time to head back?" The edge in his voice had come out of nowhere.

"I thought you said this was a circle?"

"Yup, let's go!"

With that, Jeb gave Royal a kick and took off across the open meadow. What had she said to provoke such a dramatic change in the man? She urged Tara on and the horse followed her stable mate, soon breaking into a full gallop. Amy held on for dear life.

As they reached the trailhead, he slowed down and glanced behind. "You okay?"

"*Now* you're asking? Could we take it a little slower, please?"

They rode in silence down a trail that skirted the stable's corrals. As they headed in, she noticed what appeared to be a new road branching off to the east. Curious, she called out, "Can we ride down there?"

Jeb shrugged and reined in Royal, circling back to enter the drive. She followed him round a bend where the road opened to fields and a complex of buildings, barns, bunkhouses, corrals, and a large pool area. They all looked brand-new, and it appeared that construction was ongoing.

"Wow, didn't notice this on our way in. What's is it?"

"Emma's Dream. It's a camp. It's the ranch's newest venture, brainchild of my boss, Maggie Morgan. She and her husband will run it, but we're all helping out. It's a camp for disabled kids. Where they can ride, play, and act like regular kids."

"How wonderful."

"Here's the boss man now." Jeb tipped his hat to a tall, dark-haired cowboy who stood nearby, conferring with several men in hard hats.

"Hey, Jeb, welcome back! Looking good!"

Yet another cowboy, gorgeous of course. Is there something in the water out here? Amy stared as the man approached, reminding herself to close her mouth.

"You must be Amy, Spark's daughter? Ben Morgan. Welcome." He reached up and extended his hand, which she took.

"This is quite a facility."

"My wife's dream. Happy to give you a tour when you have time. We open in three days. Twenty-five campers are comin' whether we're ready or not."

"That's so exciting. I'd love a tour, but I expect you've got your hands full right now."

Ben Morgan tipped his hat. "Always time for a pretty lady."

Jeb watched his boss and marveled at the easy way the Morgan men had with women. Ben Morgan could charm the pants off any woman he met, and he regularly did with the ranch's high-paying clientele. At the same time, Jeb knew it was just that—charm and Morgan hospitality. Ben was crazy in love with his wife, Maggie, and there was only one woman in his life. *One woman? Was Stacy my one woman?*

Morgan turned to Jeb. "You heading back to the office? Mag's comin' by with the baby pretty soon."

"So I hear. How is Ben the third?"

"Perfect, except at three a.m. His mother's threatening to come back to work, but Harley and I are going to try and convince her otherwise, at least for a few months."

"I'll be happy to join the chorus."

"Good man. I'll see you in a few. Nice to meet you, Ms. Foster."

"Same here."

Morgan tipped his hat again before turning back to the men.

*****

When they reached the corral, Jeb hopped down and came to assist her.

Not that she needed help, mind you! As his hands grasped her waist, she gazed down and their eyes met. There it was, for a second, a glimpse of attraction that he felt as much as she did. Just as quickly, it was gone, and he looked down, but still his touch was liquid fire. Amy's knees wobbled as her feet hit the ground.

"Steady now," he said, catching her under the arms.

"I'm fine." She stepped back and patted Tara's nose. "Shall I come in and rub her down?"

"No, we'll do it. You head up to the Lodge so you don't miss breakfast. They're pretty amazing."

"I don't mind."

"No trouble. We've got a bunch of kids working. They'll take care of her." He whistled, and two young teenagers emerged from the barn. "Rip, Sandy, come take these guys. I've gotta meet with the bosses."

The young men walked the horses into the barn as Jeb reached into a cooler by the corral. "Water?" he asked, holding out a bottle.

"No thanks. I'll get something at the Lodge. Don't want to keep you from your meeting."

He tipped his hat. "Okay, then."

As Jeb turned away, he willed himself not to think about the woman's silky skin and soft curves, the scent of something like honeysuckle that lingered from the few seconds when he had held her tiny waist.

Amy watched him until he disappeared into the barn. Then she turned and walked to the ridiculously huge car her dad had rented. It looked like a white whale parked alongside the bunch of trucks and dusty vehicles in the side yard. As she reached the car, a woman drove up in a dark green SUV. Curious, Amy watched as the beautiful brunette stepped out, then opened the back door and pulled out an infant car seat.

"Hello," she said, shielding her eyes as she approached, baby seat draped over one arm.

"You must be Maggie Morgan."

"And, you must be Spark's daughter. Amy?"

"Yes, hello."

The two women shook hands.

"And this must be Benjamin the third."

Maggie laughed. "The very one."

"He's adorable. I just met your husband."

"Oh? Is he here already?"

Amy shook her head. "No, we rode down to the camp. What an amazing place."

"It will be. We're really excited."

"Your husband offered to give me a tour."

"Anytime. So you said you were riding?"

"Yes, Jeb took me out."

"Oh?" Maggie's face turned serious as she set down the car seat. Worry and concern shimmered in her lovely blue eyes.

"His first day back, I understand."

"Yes," she said quietly.

"Is he okay? I mean, I don't mean to pry."

Maggie stared at her for a few seconds before replying. "I hope so. He recently lost someone very dear to him, his girlfriend. Terrible accident. Only happened four weeks ago."

"Oh, dear, how sad. I thought the scar looked new."

"Yes, he's lucky to be alive."

As the baby began to fuss, Maggie hoisted the carrier. "Well, I'd better get inside and nurse him before it's a full-blown wail. Nice to meet you, Ms. Foster."

"Amy, please."

"I expect we'll be seeing lots of each other with all the wedding festivities."

"I look forward to it."

Amy watched Maggie Morgan head to the barn, then hopped into the white whale. As she turned the ignition, she thought about Jeb's smoky sad eyes and how his touch had made her go weak in the knees. *Get a grip, Amy Foster! He's a cowboy, he's here, and you will be back in Portland in four weeks.*